D0977119

A WOLF Called WANDER

A WOLF Called WANDER

ROSANNE PARRY

ILLUSTRATIONS BY

MÓNICA ARMIÑO

Greenwillow Books
An Imprint of HarperCollinsPublishers

This book is a work of fiction. References to real people, events, establishments, organizations, or locales are intended only to provide a sense of authenticity, and are used to advance the fictional narrative. All other characters, and all incidents and dialogue, are drawn from the author's imagination and are not to be construed as real.

Map by Ryan O'Rourke
Simultaneous publication in the United Kingdom by Andersen Press Limited, 2019.

The text of this book is set in Berling Roman.
Book design by Sylvie Le Floc'h

Library of Congress Cataloging-in-Publication Data

Names: Parry, Rosanne, author. | Armiño, Mónica, illustrator.
Title: A wolf called Wander / by Rosanne Parry ; illustrated by Mónica Armiño
Description: First edition. | New York, NY : Greenwillow Books, 2019. | Summary: "A young wolf cub, separated from his pack, journeys 1000 miles across the Pacific Northwest, dealing with forest fires, hunters, highways, and hunger before finding a new home. Based on the true story of a wolf called OR-7"—Provided by publisher. Includes facts about wolves and their habitats.
Identifiers: LCCN 2018046194 | ISBN 9780062895936 (hardback)
Subjects: LCSH: Wolves—Juvenile fiction. | CYAC: Wolves—Fiction. | Animals—Infancy—Fiction. | Adventure and adventurers—Fiction. | Nature—Fiction. | BISAC: JUVENILE FICTION / Animals / Wolves & Coyotes. | JUVENILE FICTION / Action & Adventure / Survival Stories. | JUVENILE FICTION / Family / General (see also headings under Social Issues).
Classification: LCC PZ10.3.P2285 Wol 2019 | DDC [Fic]—dc23 LC record available at https://lccn.loc.gov/2018046194

19 20 21 22 23 PC/LSCH 10 9 8 7 6 5 4 3 2 1

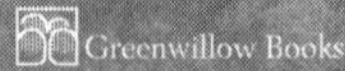
Greenwillow Books

To all who wander

in search of a home

Contents

A WOLF Called WANDER

PACK

I begin in darkness, and my nose tells me everything I know.

I have a brother. Sharp. Bigger than me, and all growl. I have sisters. Pounce, who loves to wrestle, and Wag, who talks with her tail. And best of all, my brother Warm, who likes to curl up under my chin, the only pup smaller than me.

I nose each one of them and the damp dirt above and the dry grass below. I circle the den while the others drowse. I take test runs up the tunnel. They call me Swift because I was the first to stand up and walk. Wherever my legs take me,

I always circle back to the empty hollow spot in the center of the den that smells like home, like the thing I can never smell enough. And then she comes in out of the wind, the best of all smells: Mother.

She turns around once, nose-touching each of us in turn, and then lies down in her hollow. Sharp, Pounce, and Wag dive for her belly to drink. I could have been first, but Mother's fur is full of smells. From her hip to her shoulder to her warm growly breath, she holds smells with no name. Smells that make me want to push beyond the place at the mouth of the tunnel where Mother has said, "Do not pass," and put my nose where the light comes from.

I am late for lunch. Warm creeps toward the last drinking spot. I lunge for it. And then—ahhh—drinking fast and strong, drinking gulps and dribbles and gasps. Mother sings to us as we drink, about the wide world beyond our den and the story of our life in the mountains. I take in her song like air, like milk—pack, mountains, elk, stars, wind, rain, howl, hunt, mountains, pack.

As always, Warm squirms under me in his low-to-the-ground way. He whimpers and pushes his head under my chin. Pop! My drinking spot is gone. Belly half full, I move on. I do not even try Sharp. He is big, and there is a bite behind all that loudmouth yowling. I nudge Pounce, but she steps on my head. Wag gives up her drinking spot when I push her away. Wag pushes Pounce, who pushes Sharp, and then he turns to Warm, teeth bared, and growls the one word we all know.

"Mine!"

Warm creeps away and curls up in the back of the den alone. One by one we slide full-bellied into dreams. Before I do, I catch a sweet smell that gives me no peace. I yawn, lift my nose, and . . . yes. Yes, there is more milk. And I can claim it. More, and if I drink it, I will grow to be even bigger than Sharp. I find just one swallow in every drinking spot. And now I know one thing my brothers and sisters do not: hind milk is the sweetest of all. I lick the last drops from my chin and curl my body around Warm so they will not step on him in the dark.

"Tell me again," I say to Mother. I point my nose to the tunnel. "When can I go outside?"

"It's wild and hungry out there on the home ground," Mother says. "And you are tender and tasty, my wolfling, my own. Wait until you are bigger."

She sighs at the soft pool of light that has spilled through the Do Not Pass onto the den floor.

"Wait until you have a fighting chance."

I stretch my nose toward the light and stifle the yawn that comes with the stretch. I don't want to wait. My sisters and brothers breathe the slow, deep breaths of sleep. My head bobs, but I fight.

"Tell me more."

"The pack belongs to the mountains and the mountains belong to the pack," she begins. "And the wolf star shines on us all."

I listen, but the long and winding slide into dreams carries me away.

And so I sleep and wake and eat and sleep, until the time when I wake and Mother is gone. A cool white glow shines in from the Do Not Pass. I check on all five smells of us and the dirt and the dry grass and the echo of Mother's smell in her hollow. Everything is here. Everything is right.

Except my empty belly. I feel the sway of it side to side as I pace the den floor. There is less room now. No new smells to smell, only longer bodies to trip over, and Sharp is still the biggest of us all.

Mother has never left us so long. Warm whimpers and rubs his head along my shoulder.

"The pack belongs to the mountains. The mountains belong to the pack," Wag says.

"And the wolf star shines on us all," Warm chimes in.

They go on, the two of them, telling each other the story.

Sharp pretends not to care that Mother is gone, but he puts his teeth on Pounce, just in case she might taste good. She wrestle-stomps him to the ground. I take my nose to the Do Not Pass to learn what a pup can know.

Warm shivers at the dare I am taking. I don't care. I am only a paw length over the line. Two paws over. Three! Three paws over the line and I can smell new things. The dark den of the sky has a soft white circle that glows. Smaller white sparks flicker all around it. So many of them. More than tails, more than paws, more even than claws, paws, and tails together. I cannot stop watching them.

The cool air carries news of faraway things I have only heard about in stories: pine, mouse, owl, fir, huckleberry, water. There is more in the air than I can name.

I inch forward against Warm's nudge of warning.

"Do not pass!"

Crouch. Freeze. It is a new wolf.

Sniff. Freeze. It is a not-Mother smell.

Sniff. Wag. Freeze.

I've smelled him on Mother's fur. He is kin. I creep forward.

"Do not pass!"

Warm is long gone to the back of the den, but I can't keep the wag out of my tail. It thwaps on the den roof and rains down dirt.

"Hush!"

Nose to ground. I do not mean to bow down. His voice pulls me down.

"Listen," he says, not so harsh this time.

My ears turn. The wind brings sound along with smell.

Whoosh, creak, pop from the wind in the trees nearby. Hoot and scurry from farther off. And then howl.

Hoooooowl. My fur goes up all over. It is a sound from my dreams. I feel an answering howl deep inside, but not so deep that the pup-watcher can't see it about to come out.

"Hush," he says. "Hush!"

I swallow my howl and sit on my wag. I wait, hunger forgotten, in the wash of new sounds. The pup-watcher waits too. He paces slowly, a gray shape in a circle of trees.

I hear water running far away, buzz and chirp-chirp from nearby. The heartbeat sound of running feet from medium far. And then nearer. And nearer still. And now I can smell them: Mother and our kin.

Sharp, Wag, and Pounce are all at my heels now. They crowd in beside me, stepping over Warm and making hungry whimpers. And then Mother comes over the ridge. Running. With the pack all around her.

Mother! She is silver-gray, and tall with black ears and a black tail tip. Her kin rub shoulders with her. They bow their heads and sing her name. I can smell her sweet-wild, milk-wind smell.

"Come," she says.

I am all wag. "Outside?" I want to be sure.

"Come," she says. "Come out."

I spring up, but Sharp shoulders past me, and Pounce steps on my hind end. I roll her off, and we burst out of the den together, raining dirt on Wag and Warm behind us.

I am out. Out! The bigness of it, this new den with the black roof no jump could reach. I jump anyway, just to try. Wind runs through my fur. My kin nose me from head to tail. I breathe in each one of them: golden-furred Song, the hunter, and the pup-watcher Growl, who walks slowly and with a limp. I cannot stop the wag. I lick the ground of our gathering place: salt, iron, ash. Home.

Father stands above the rest, gray face, black ears, and tall, tall, tall. His scent-mark is on the doorway of our den. His is the howl the pack follows. I know I should go to him and share smells, but he is silent and tall.

Sharp beats me to it. He brushes past. He is a head taller than me, and he looks down on me just to show that he can. His tail is up as always, but it goes down when he gets close to Father. He ducks his head and slows to a creep. Father gives him two sniffs and a growl and nudges him away.

Sharp turns to the rest of us, teeth

snapping, a growl in his throat, warning us that he is the one to smell-share with Father, not us. Warm cries a little. Wag says nothing, but the hopeful lift of her tail droops. Pounce takes the bait and wrestles Sharp to the ground, losing twice before she pins him.

I slip by them all and go to meet my father, tall-tailed and nose up. But as I get close, my tail drops like a stone. I almost turn back to bring Warm along, for courage, but some things a pup has to do on his own.

Up close, Father is not just gray and black but golden on the chest and silvered over the shoulders. Dark red runs around his mouth.

"Son," he growls to me. "Mine."

I sit on my wag, but it will not hold still. I breathe in the smell of him, deeper and longer until his scent holds a spot in my memory right next to Mother. I will do anything for him! I jump-spin, hoping he will like it. I yip-wag.

"Father! Mine!"

I cannot stop smelling the red on him. It makes me hungry like the smell of Mother's milk, but this is a new smell. A richer smell. I can't resist it. I nose his chin. I lick his face. He leans toward me and opens his mouth wide.

A great red and runny lump comes out of his mouth. It steams. It is nothing I have ever smelled before. But Father gave it to me.

Sniff? Sniff!

The more I smell it, the more I like it. I push my nose into the pile and rub it into my fur. Mother calls the other pups and lowers her mouth to their licking. She pushes another red lump of something out of her mouth.

She nudges Wag and Pounce to try it. Aunt Song does the same for Sharp and Warm. I turn back to Father's gift.

Lick-lick-lick.

It tastes smooth and rich. Not so sweet as milk but tail-wagging good all the same.

Nibble? Nibble.

The lumps are thick and chewy.

Bite-bite-gobble-gobble-gobble-gulp. *Ahhhhhhh!*

The rest of the pups join in, hind ends all a-wag. I eat until I am dizzy-full and curl up in Father's shadow as sleep stalks me. Father noses me into place at his feet.

"Elk," he says. "Life of the pack."

WATCH

All summer the pack hunts. Growl watches us while they are gone. When the pack comes home, there are steaming piles of elk meat for everyone and then, best of all, howling. Father begins and then Mother and then Song. The sound of it makes my fur stand up and my tail wave. We pups howl together, each trying to be the loudest, stretching our necks out and up like Father does. We draw in deep breaths to win the longest howl or the loudest. But loud or soft, long or short, our howling makes us a pack. All of us, one pack, and this our home ground. Our voices bounce off the mountains. They reach for the wolf star. The sound fills me up like fresh water.

Growl sounds his low, mournful wails last of all. He is the following wolf, our wrestling coach, and the peacemaker of the pack. By the time the meadow turns late-summer gold I can outrun him, and by the first frost I can make him drop his tail when I beat the ground with my front paws and raise the fur on my shoulders.

Sharp never drops his tail to me, no matter how hard I try. I wrestle him every day, but he slips out of my paws. I run farther than him. I howl longer. I gulp down more meat than anyone, but he is still taller and heavier, louder and stronger. I can run faster than him, but that is my only victory. Mother sees me try and gives me extra licks at sleep time.

"A lead wolf feeds his pack," she says. "No other trick matters."

So when the first snow falls, instead of snapping at snowflakes and skidding over frozen puddles with the rest of the pups, I run with Father to the game-watching place. It takes all my strength to keep up, but I am stronger every day. When we arrive at the flat stone by the home stream, I sit at his feet. He studies the mountainside. And I watch him watching.

He hears the yowl of cougars and the yip of coyotes and the rattling call of ravens. He hears running water, the splash, grunt, huff of the bear, and the split, splat of the salmon hitting the stones on the side of the river. And then the long, contented tear and chew of a bear eating fish. I listen to him listening.

An orange-bellied squirrel runs from the base of one tree to another. It is fast, but I am faster.

"Can I hunt it, Father?" I get in my crouch, ready to spring.

"Can you?"

I am all leap. In a flicker the squirrel is around the back of the tree and I have crashed into the front. I slide down the trunk as the squirrel goes higher and higher, springing from branch to branch like a bird. I shake the bark bits out of my fur.

Father does not laugh at me. But he wags a little.

I sit down again and watch my father watch the mountains. The wind blows. Birds talk to each other.

"There, Father! Right there!"

A short-legged weasel thing walks across the stream below us. It is black as night with a broad white stripe from neck to tail and a narrow white stripe down the nose. It is plump. It will be delicious.

"I could hunt it. I know I could."

My spring is ready to go. Two jumps and I will have him. Father slaps a paw down on my shoulder and presses me flat to the ground.

"What has your mother said about eating white things?"

"White berries," I say, trying to squirm out of his grasp. "White mushrooms. Never touch them, not even a lick."

I tug and turn, but he will not let me up. He watches me struggle. I am not even making him tired. I huff and puff and pull and strain and finally roll over and lift my chin to surrender.

He lets me go.

I spring to my feet, nose pointing at my prey. "That is not a berry. It is not a mushroom. It is walking!"

"Yes, walking. In plain sight. Showing us a white stripe—and no fear. What is that animal telling you?"

I lower my nose and tail.

"Poison?"

"Worse than poison."

I flop back down in the dust and drop my chin to my paws.

"I could catch it, though. I could get it all by myself."

"Not. Even. A. Lick."

I look up at my father. He is not laughing at me, except for that little wag. I go over to the weasel thing's tracks and learn their five-toed shape. Not-Lunch waddles slowly, almost teasing, off into the forest. I feel like whimpering, but then I remember to hold it in and sit up tall. Who needs to eat? Not me.

I sit beside my father. More watching. The shadows go long, and he is still watching. The rest of the pups have been playing all day, but Father is still watching. My wag is long gone, but I am with him, still watching.

A scuffle of noise at the edge of the waterfall catches my eye. A black nose peeks out, followed by the most wild-haired weasel ever. Its hairs are long and stiff and wave out in all directions. It is even slower than the last one. I could catch that thing. I look at Father. He is not crouching to stalk it. He is looking at me.

"Is it delicious?" I nose-point to the weasel.

"Probably."

The thing goes to a pine tree and nibbles at the bark. The stiff thick hairs are silver-gray at the tips and black at the base.

"Is it poisonous?"

"No." He wags—just a little.

I make a little yip in case it hasn't smelled us watching so nearby. It turns and doesn't back away. Badgers and wolverines are not big, but Mother has warned us about them.

"Does that thing hunt us?"

"Nothing hunts a grown wolf but men."

"He is so small. Why is he not afraid?"

"The porcupine fears no one and fights no one."

"But I could get him in one pounce. He is so slow."

"Anyone who tangles with a porcupine bows to him forever after."

No way am I bowing to that thing. I watch it slowly and clumsily climbing the pine tree. There is nothing sleek or strong or shrewd about it. I will get Sharp to tangle with it. Then I will know, and Sharp will have to do the bowing.

The wind dies down and the sun sinks even lower. Ravens come. They circle Father and go out toward the prairie. They circle back, and Father woofs to them as though they can talk. They swoop around him again, so close their long black wing tips stir the fur on his shoulders. Off they go again, back to the prairie.

"There!" Father says, nose-pointing to open ground

below, where the prairie grasses meet up with the trees and ferns of the mountainside. I look and see nothing. Father calls for Mother and Song. I lift my head to smell and faintly it comes to me—a deer and her pup. Mother and Song run to Father's side.

I watch it all: the quick and silent approach, the line of attack, the direction of the wind, the way my father circles around the front, turning the deer back into the jaws of Mother and Song. In my head I'm there with them, chasing, circling, springing. I will feed my pack. I will. Better than all of them.

I watch Father hunt every day. Even after I grow from a pup to a yearling. I learn. I remember. I run. Run just to feel the wind in my fur and the pound of my feet on the sweet grass and soft needles of my home ground. Sometimes Warm runs behind me, and sometimes I practice-hunt him. We work on my stalk, my chase, my spring. He is the perfect following wolf, far better than I could ever be. I will be a lead wolf; I can feel it.

RIVAL

As the last heat of summer fades, Mother teaches Pounce and Wag to dig a den. I watch them go and remember the porcupine. Now is my chance.

"Sharp, I found something to hunt."

"Is it elk?"

"Something better."

"If it's not elk, I'm not interested."

"Warm and I can do it by ourselves, then." I turn away, tail held tall, and Warm walks away with me.

"Do not look back," I say under my breath.

There is a scramble of running paws, then the two quick steps that come before a pounce. I roll to the side. Sharp hits the dirt. I love it when that happens. My joy is short-lived. With a growl and a snap, he pins me to the ground.

"Where do you think you're going without me?"

I squirm and tug and push, but I can't work myself free. With a huff of disgust I show my throat to him, and he lets me up.

"Swift and I can hunt without you," Warm says. He sits down to stop his wag.

"Oh no you don't," Sharp says. "I've got this one."

It is all going better than I planned.

"Over by the watching spot," I say. "By the stand of pines."

Sharp takes the lead, all swagger. Warm and I follow at a respectful distance. Neither of us can hold in the wag. We come to the spot where Father watches the mountains, and we both hear it at the same time—ravens, a whole cloud of them. We look out over the prairie. Vultures circle above the ravens. Someone has made a kill. But Father and Mother are not hunting today. I look beneath the cloud of birds, and there are wolves, many of them.

"We should tell—"

Warm is already gone. In a few heartbeats he and Mother are by my side. Looking. Pacing.

"Will we leave?" Warm says. "Should we go?"

Every time I look, there seem to be more wolves on the prairie. My heart sinks. Mother turns. She fixes me with her amber gaze, and I cannot look away. I stand taller. Pounce and Wag stand on either side of me. Sharp lifts himself up, a full head taller than the rest of us. I nudge Warm into place.

"We belong to the mountains," Mother begins.

"And the mountains belong to us," we reply.

"Look at you—all grown," she says. "What do I have to fear, with such wolves for my own? Stay here. Father and I will mark our borders."

They run off together to wet-mark the trees at the edge of our home ground, to send a message to any who would cross. When they come back we have a howl—such a howl! Loud and long into the night. We push the stranger wolves away with our song as the first chill of winter whistles down our mountains.

A few days later, when the yellow and brown leaves are thick on the ground and the wind has biting teeth and the home stream is silver and slippery at the edges, Father calls us to our first hunt. Before, we followed the pack and waited in the trees, breathless, as our betters brought down elk. Hunters ate first, but then we charged in for our share.

"Come," Father says. "We are many wolves now, and the elk are fewer than they have been."

Father leads us to a broad open meadow between two rocky ridges with an iced-over stream running through. We stop on the windward side, where the herd cannot smell us. The elk kick at the snow where it's shallow to uncover the last frosty stalks of grass. They nibble at shrubs.

"We must run them first to see who stumbles," Father says. "I will run on the sunrise side of the herd with Sharp and Wag. Mother and Song and Pounce will run on the other."

My tail drops to the ground. He does not want me in the hunt. I will never be a lead wolf if I cannot take down meat.

"Warm, you stay on the high ground and keep the herd from running upstream," he says.

Warm bristles out his golden-gray fur with pride. It is an easy job. Elk would rather run downhill than up. But it is help to the pack.

"Swift, you run ahead of us and cover the low ground. Turn them uphill. The more we can make them turn, the easier it will be to make one stumble."

Yes! I stifle a yelp, but I am all wag. I can outrun the whole pack. Everyone knows. I bump shoulders with Sharp and bite his ears to say so. I will pay for that later, but I do not care. This is my chance. If I do better than him in the hunt, he will never step on me again—or Warm either.

Father nose-points us into our places above the snowy meadow where elk are browsing unaware. The wind blows toward us hard and cold. The hunt is a fire inside me. I will be the wolf to feed my family. I crouch in the shadow of trees and wait

for Father's signal. In all the hunts I have watched, victory came when the pack burst on to the herd like one sweep of the wind.

And then, with no signal from Father, Sharp leaps into the open and lets out a yip. The whole herd looks right at him.

"Go!" Father growls to me.

It is too late to scold. We are one pack in victory and one in loss. I charge into the meadow, furious. I will not accept loss on my first hunt. Drifts of snow at the meadow's edge churn up around my shoulders. Warm veers uphill. No harm will come to him there. Mother takes her hunters around one side of the herd, and Father takes his around

the other. I stretch out my run. Faster. Downhill.

I see Sharp take a flying leap at the very first elk in his reach. He misses. Sharp is all pup, all wrestle and impatience. I will pin him to the ground later if it takes me a thousand tries. He does not even look to see if his elk is staggering. Father only watches the elk's legs, nothing else. When he finds an elk off its stride, he will move in for the kill.

The elk gallop through the snow, dodging away from the deepest drifts at the edge, leaping over the patches of ice in the middle. Their high-pitched sounds of panic echo around us. I run hard to gain the head of the herd and turn them back uphill. The first elk shies away from me, and then another. The rest follow. I can hear Father and Growl running behind me. I catch a glimpse of Mother and Song through a forest of running legs. A tall elk with many points on his rack bursts past me. I let him go. He is too fine a creature to catch. I make the rest of the herd turn and then run back to make them turn again.

Sharp has shaken off his mistake. He is bounding along at Father's heels. On the third turn, Father sees an elk break stride. He jumps for the throat. I let the rest of the herd go.

Father's teeth are deep into the shaggy black fur at the elk's neck. I can taste victory. I run to give my father aid, but Sharp is many strides ahead of me. He leaps at the elk's shoulder and sinks his teeth into the crown of the neck. Father loses his grip from the force of Sharp's blow. Not even Mother and Song are fast enough. By the time I am in place to spring, the elk is already dead.

"Well hunted," Father says to Sharp.

We stand in a ring around the elk. Breathing hard. Thankful for the life that gives us life. Everyone eats, and everyone is eaten, Growl used to say to us when we were pups. And so we take a moment to be grateful that we are the ones eating this time. Then we step back while Father and Mother take their first share, the rest of us panting and yipping with glee at the smell of fresh meat.

Song is always second to eat, and then us yearlings and then Growl.

But this time, Father brings Sharp to the food before Song and says nothing when he gobbles down all the choicest bits. By the time it is my turn, there is almost nothing left but nibbles and bone. I crack open a long leg bone and lick out the center. It fills me up, but I leave the meal unsatisfied and more determined than ever to beat my brother. We turn back to our gathering place at nightfall, leaving the scraps of our kill for raccoons and slinking coyotes.

All winter long we hunt, filling our bellies, leaving red-stained snow and scraps for scavengers behind. All winter Father chooses me to run the herd, and Sharp to help him make the kill. I can run circles around them all, but Sharp is still the biggest. We are yearlings, but he is as tall as Father, and if he keeps getting first go at the meat, he will be as big as Father soon. I am not the bringer of meat. Maybe I never will be. I grow restless as the season turns.

I stop following Father to the watching spot and find my own place away from our family meeting ground. I turn my face to the setting sun and watch the wide-open prairie, with its herds of elk and cows and sheep. Warm joins me, curling up under my chin, so that I can hear his heart beating in time with mine. This is my home ground. I love every stream and stand of trees. But Sharp always wins, and I do not want to be his following wolf.

"Take me with you when you go," Warm says.

I growl in answer, not yes, but not no. I lick his ears where Sharp and Pounce like to bite. Summer is coming again, and we will be yearlings no more. Mother has been in the den for the full circle of a moon. Growl is weaker than before and needs to be fed like a pup. My pack needs me. I could never leave them.

"I would follow you anywhere," Warm says.

FIGHT

When the last of the snow has melted and the sun makes its slow summer walk across the sky, new pups come out of the den, jumping at every little cricket and singing to every mountain sparrow. In the joy of watching them, we watch our borders less.

On the first full moon of summer, we are all gathered on the home ground, giving elk from our mouths to our pups. They are all wag and happy licking. Mother watches over them with pride, and Warm is right in the thick of them, rolling and wrestling and always, always he circles the group, making sure that none stray.

The ravens have joined us in the light of the moon, howling their own harsh songs and bowing to their own alpha bird. They snap up stray bits of meat. Toss bones in the air and dive for them. This is how wolves should live.

I have a favorite pup already, the dark brown one with the black tail tip who keeps getting stepped on by her bigger sister. I woof at her to stand up when her big sister knocks her down. I guard her share of the meat.

I should have been listening. We all should have.

It is Warm who smells them first. He gives a warning yip. All heads turn, ears swiveling back and forth. One sharp whistle from the leader of ravens, and the birds go silent. They lift into the air in one motion and are gone.

Trouble is coming.

A mist rises up the mountains, muffling sounds and cutting off our sight. Mother stands, and the pups tumble over each other to hide behind her. A growl gathers at the back of her throat. I lift my nose to test the wind. The night air is completely still, and all I can smell is the meat right in front of us. Song goes to Mother and stands guard, nose to tail and teeth bared. Wag and Pounce look to Father for commands.

An enemy pack steps out of the trees, a circle of wolves as pale as weathered wood, and broad shouldered. They are many. Enough to surround us easily. Enough to take us and all our pups, if we do not drive them away. They speak in snarls, and their ice-blue eyes say, "Mine!"

Father rises up, tall and mighty. The enemy wolves are many, but he is strong. Mother sprints up

the mountain, calling the pups to follow. She winds through trees, scrambles over rocks, and leaps our home stream. The pups follow in line. Growl hides his limp and roars at the intruders, as menacing as any bear. I stand shoulder to shoulder with Sharp and Pounce, Wag and Song, making a barrier the enemy pack will have to break to harm our pups.

"Follow them," I yip to Warm. "Keep them safe."

Our pups are young, but Warm will never let them fall. He whirls and runs after them, as swift and silent as the owl flies in the dark.

We snarl. Anger gives me a surge of strength. I do not care how big they are. This is my home ground. They will not have it. I leap at a stranger with all my strength. She doesn't go down. I rear up again, and she tumbles me over. I sink my teeth into her leg. She tears at my ear. I hold and hold and hold and twist until I hear a snap of bone. She gives a yelp of surrender, and I let her scramble away.

The rest circle Father, lunging, biting. Red runs out of him. The enemy leader is not as big as Father, but he is fierce. His pack is notch-eared and relentless. They circle us like we circle a herd of elk. They look for the weak wolf. They look for fear. Growl is already on the ground, back twisted, legs not moving. They lunge all together for Father. We dive in to pull the attackers off. Two of the smaller ones fall, but there are many more.

An enemy wolf breaks away from the fight and smells the ground. If he finds the pups' trail, they will be lost. I dash after him. The pale wolf is thick with muscle. I cannot win, but I can draw him away from my family. I give a weak yelp. Let him think I am an easy catch. Mother went up the mountain, so I go down. I circle back. I leap the home stream, and the enemy wolf follows.

In a blur I see the fight as I run past. Father holds his ground. Sharp makes a yelp. He runs on three legs toward the den. If the pale wolf sees Sharp, he will take him, just as we always take the elk who stumbles. But if Sharp can hide, he might have a chance.

I make a low-tail sound like Warm makes when Pounce bullies him. I swerve away from Sharp, and the pale wolf follows me, leaving my brother alone. The enemy wolf is fast, but I am on my home ground. I know the smooth hard places and where to leap badger holes and anthills. He is too strong to fight, but I can make him fall.

I turn down the steepest, rockiest ground, but he follows. Follows so close, I feel breath on my heels. I spin to one side, leading him into a mound of biting ants. He blazes through them without breaking stride. I dodge around shrubs. Duck between trees. No matter where I turn, he's right there, snarling and snapping at my tail. I head for the deep pool at a bend in the river. If I can make him slip on the rocks, I can roll his head underwater and hold him there. Moonlight betrays me. He sees the pool and bounds over it.

Desperate, I lead him to the downed trees from last summer's fire. They are charred black and thick as a hawthorn bramble. I dive into the tangle of timbers. Black twigs break in my fur. I turn and shift and squeeze into the darkest spaces, where the pale wolf can't fit. I squirm through the middle and then run

along the top of a narrow log. It takes me to the edge of the downed trees, where I can jump free into the long meadow below. I gather myself and leap for open ground.

The pale wolf follows along the same log, crouches to make the same jump. But the log gives way with a snap. He falls, yelping, backward, onto the spikes of broken tree trunks. He lands with a thud, and nothing but silence comes from the body.

Yes! I leap for joy. My victory. My kill.

I whirl around and run back. I will lure another wolf away and another. They are only winning because they are many. I can save my pack. A lead wolf defends his family. It is the only thing that matters more than food.

I am only halfway home when I hear, carried on the wind from deep in my home ground, my father's last song. All creatures have one at the end. Even the silent rabbit screams.

My father's song is short and high. It echoes from the stones.

"Carry on. Carry on. Carry on . . ."

My fur stands up and I lift my head for one last—one very last—smell of him. But I am far and all I can smell is the enemy wolf and all I can hear is the enemy pack answering, drowning out my father's song with their chant.

"Mine! Mine!"

I turn toward the sunset and run like water runs from the mountains. My paws pound over the ground, and Father's last song pounds in my heart.

Carry on. Carry on. Carry on.

ELK

The sun rises behind me, and I am still running. The trees thin to nothing. The ground goes flat. I could run until the earth meets the sky, but the smell of water calls me. I veer from my course to a shallow pool ringed with reeds and shrubs. I smell the wind for dangers, but there is nothing at all.

As I drink, the nothing I smell and hear and see weighs me down like stones. Father is gone. Growl too. But what of the rest? Did Warm find a place to hide? Did Mother and the pups? Did the survivors scatter? They could be anywhere.

I pace the edge of the water. I want to call them.

Need to call them. But to survive, they must hide. I raise my nose to the wind, but there is no smell of anything but grass and water. A pack of birds, as brown and yellow as the tall grass around them, flits from one stalk to the next. They sing as if nothing has happened. I snap at one, and the whole pack of them swoops up and away.

I turn my ears in every direction. Wind. Bees. The rustle of mice through the grass. The whisper of a snake following. I turn a full circle twice.

I am alone.

Should I go and find them? Wait here by the water? The air will be cooler come night. It will carry a smell better. I curl up in the tall grass, tucking my tail in for comfort, but my heart pounds as though I am at a dead run.

I used to go off on my own. In the mountains there was always something beautiful just over the next ridge—a lake, a berry field, a sheltered patch of ice. But I always came home to my family. I have never, not once in my life, slept alone.

The weary day goes on and on, and nobody comes. They could be anywhere—in the forest on the far side of the mountain . . . deep in the river canyon. I circle again and again—listening, smelling. The sky darkens, and my pack does not come. Stars come out, and I can smell no one. And then a full moon rises, and the pale wolves begin to howl. First the leader, and then another, howls in, and another and another. I lose count of them. Their voices are strange and wild and mean. And then, at the very end of their song, Sharp gives a low and whimpering howl. He is their following wolf now, and no brother of mine. If any of my pack live, they are silent or gone.

The wolf star, brightest of all in the summer sky, shines over my home ground. I know every hidden lake and rocky ridge, but if my pack is not in the mountains, then it is no home to me. I feel a howl deep inside but dare not let it out.

In the morning I wake with a start. I can smell Warm. I spring to my feet and raise my nose to the wind.

The smell is gone.

But I did smell something. I dreamed of Warm sleeping curled up under my chin as he always does. Singing his quiet songs. I dash over to a rise in the ground and sample the breeze again.

Maybe I was wrong. There is no smell from a footfall. He has not walked past. But there is a very faint wolf smell carried on the wind, mixed in with the nip of pinesap and sweet mountain flowers. It could be him. He would follow me anywhere; he promised. But he would keep our pups safe first.

I spring up and run for my home ground. I will find him, and the pups too. I will save them all. The ground rises. I keep searching. I stop. Breathe in. Turn in a full circle. I hold my breath with listening.

It is gone. But it was there. I know it was. I keep going. Hoping that Warm found a way to slip through the enemy pack, hoping Mother and the pups found a place to hide. No wolf knows our mountains like Mother. I run until the shadow of them falls over me. Still nothing. I trot to one side and then the other. Listening. Tasting the air.

And then it hits me like a rock falling from a ledge—the border-mark of the pale wolf pack. I can see where they have stood and claw-marked the bark in long slashes as high as they can reach, where they have wet the tree trunks. The smell turns my stomach over. These were my trees. My meadows. My cold streams and ice-capped peaks. But the border-mark stops me like the face of a cliff. I must not pass.

I cannot leave Warm to the teeth and claws of the intruders. I wet-mark a tree on my side of the border. I beat the ground with my paws, laying down a scent he can follow. I run along the prairie side of the border and wet-mark the scattered oaks and aspen as I go. I cannot kill the pale wolves, but I can light a path for Warm to find me.

The prairie is hotter than the forest and more colorful. Blue and purple and red flowers nod in the wind. They hum with bees, and everywhere I step there is a grasshopper or beetle scuttling away from my paw. As the heat of the day comes on, I climb a butte and stake a lookout for Warm, for any survivor of my pack.

Way over by the canyon rim I see elk. Good. When I find my family, we will need to hunt. The broad-winged hawk with the rust-colored tail turns slow circles in the sky, and the little hawk with the speckled wings hovers and strikes at mice. All afternoon I watch and listen. Black-and-white cows and their pups browse the grass. As the shadows lengthen, the pack of cows moves along and sheep wander through the shrubs at the foot of my butte. They are slow and have ugly voices. I am about to head back for water when I smell them—wolves!

I run to the edge of the butte's flat top. It is not Warm. There are at least two wolves, by the smell of things. They are not my pack. They could be hunters from the enemy pack, scouts looking to kill every last one of us. I crouch-freeze among the boulders. In leaving a path for Warm, I have led the pale wolves straight to me. I am certain I can outrun any single wolf, but nobody can outrun a whole pack.

I watch their approach. There are two. Only two.

They are not tracking my path as they come. They are stalking prey. I am dizzy with relief when I see, by their dark brown and boulder-gray coats, that they are not the enemy pack. These wolves are young, like me, and male. I listen and wait for the rest of their pack to join the hunt, but no one else comes.

They must be on their own. Yearling bachelors. They drop into the waiting-to-hunt crouch with their eyes fixed on sheep—coyote food. Father never fed us sheep. I look from one wolf to the other to see which is the leader. They both carry their tails tall. They are both inching ahead to be the first to spring. This is not going to go well.

The brown wolf springs first, but the sheep ducks to the side, whirls free, and runs screaming across the prairie. The gray wolf springs a moment too late and only manages to grab a hind leg in his teeth. He holds on to the kicking sheep as all the rest run away. The brown wolf turns back and drives home the killing bite.

Afterward, there is no nod to thank the lead wolf, no pause to honor the life of the meat. Both wolves tear through the skin, spilling guts in the dirt and dragging the choicest bits of food from each other's mouths. A disgusting thing to see. No order in the pack. No respect. Maybe they are orphans. They must have learned to hunt from watching coyotes.

I turn away from them and look to my mountains. Mother and the pups could have escaped. They could be on the far side of the mountains. Warm and Song, maybe even Pounce or Wag, could be with them. They could be out on a prairie somewhere, hunting elk like wolves should. Mother would never abandon her pups. She would defend them to her death. We all would.

Hunger wakes me at dawn. A vulture is picking over the remains of the sheep the bachelor wolves left behind. The wolves are long gone, and I want no part of them. They are no better than the skulking coyotes that came in the dark to pick over our scraps and slink away before sunrise.

Elk were on the horizon yesterday. That is what Father would want me to hunt. If any of my pack survived, that is where they will be. I set aside my hunger and run.

Even with my sorrows, running is all joy. There are no trees or windfalls or ravines to dodge around.

I run flat out, the ground pounding under my paws. If my family is alive, they will be near the elk. The smell of elk grows stronger. I lift my nose as I run, to search for some scent of my pack.

I circle around to where the elk can't smell me. My family would gather here and wait for the right moment. I slow to a trot. Stop.

Nothing.

I circle back. Bark a call. A prairie full of food

is waiting for us, but my pack is gone. I bark out another call and another.

No one calls back.

They cannot be gone. Not all of them. Grass and shrubs spread before me as broad as the sky. How will I ever find them? Hunger beats me to the ground, and I lie in the grass, wishing for the cool shade, the soft moss and needles of my home ground. The size of the sky makes me feel small, and I long for the company of trees.

Over the open ground come the voices of elk; their relaxed whines and whistles tell me they have not caught wind that I am here. Even though I am thirsty, water runs from my mouth at the sound of them. I will hunt. I must. And when I've brought down meat, my pack will come. They will see the ravens and vultures gather; they will hear coyotes sing my praises; and they will find me.

The elk are far, but I am fast. I run for them, not caring that I am spending speed before I should. I will feed my pack. Nothing else matters.

They hold their position at first, but soon the mother elk standing guard barks the call to run. Pups mother up. They move together toward the sunset. I do not care. No one can run like me. I gain on them steadily until the beat of hooves on the ground is all I can hear, and elk sweat and fear is all I can smell.

The pups bleat in full panic. I find an elk that is falling behind and mark him as mine. I can taste the meat already. I will take this elk down, and Warm will find me. Mother and the rest will come running from wherever they are hiding. We will be a pack again, and this will be our new home ground.

I run alongside the elk as Father did. He would pick a moment to leap and make a killing blow. I have seen him do it, but I always ran in front and turned the herd. There is no one to turn them for me now. Hunger drives me to run faster, to get out in front of the elk and turn him, so that I can make the killing strike. The others swerve away, and my mark comes to a dead stop, bellowing in anger and waving his head from side to side. I check my run and circle back, only to have the elk turn again. In less than a heartbeat he kicks, slicing deep into the meat of my chest.

My breath whooshes out. I hear the crack of bone. Fire runs up my neck and down to the pads of my feet. I hit the ground, and night falls as swift as a thunderclap.

PAIN

Darkness clears like a lifting fog. Pain is bone-deep in my shoulder. I lift my head, and the prairie grass shimmers around me like water. My head drops back to the ground, and darkness swallows me again.

In my dreams I am fighting an enemy pack I cannot see, but when I fight free and open my eyes, I am alone. The throb in my chest aches with every breath. I cannot feel one paw. I push at it with my nose, but it will not move. I lick it, but no warmth comes. The elk are nowhere in sight. Red drips into a pool under my shoulder. I look-smell all around. The elk are long gone. One vulture makes broad circles above me. Hunger makes my head swim. I lick at my hurt. I am so thirsty I lap up the entire pool of red. I long for my den, for the shelter of trees. I turn my face to the mountains and remember my home ground.

When I wake, I smell a wolf again. Just one, and it is far from me. I desperately want it to be Warm. I need it to be a wolf from my pack. Someone who will find me and help me grow strong again. Not an enemy wolf, who will kill me on sight. Not one of those bachelor wolves, who might kill me if he had the chance. If they are low enough to eat sheep, they just might. But there is a thought worse than being killed. They might find me and then walk away because I am no pack mate of theirs. I might have done the same just a few sunrises ago. Not now. Now I know what it means to be alone.

Night has fallen, and I am hungrier and weaker than before. When I lift my head, pain runs like lightning from my shoulder to my paw. The smell of a wolf is still in the air. Faintly. So very faintly. I brace myself to stand, but only my back legs will bear weight. It could be Warm, my Warm, all alone in the night, just like me. I should find him. I should help him. The stars are bright, and the moon rests on the horizon like an egg in a nest. I take a breath. Try to stand again. I call to Warm that I am coming. Beg him to wait for me. The edges of my hurt shoulder split open, and red pours out again. I slump, dizzy and heartsick, in the dirt.

I lie still and watch the stars. They move across the sky as steady and slow as elk graze across the prairie. The wolf smell fades from the air. When it is gone, completely gone, I whimper for my brother like a newborn pup.

In the dark of night, I wake with a start. A wolf has walked by me while I slept. A female wolf. Not Mother. Not Wag or Pounce or Song. She came to me in the night. She walked all around me. Looked at me. Smelled me. There is a tuft of black hair and a print of her paw in the dust. A prickle of fear rises along my neck and shoulders. She could be a scout from the enemy pack. Even now she could be bringing them here to kill me. I try to remember the smells of the pale wolves. My memory of that day is a blur of snarling teeth and claws soaked in red. I do not remember a black wolf among them.

I shiver from nose to tail. I cannot run from them. My one strength, and in my hour of need it has abandoned me. I will never call myself Swift again. I search out the wolf star that hangs faithfully over my home ground. I can only hope, and face whatever comes with all the fight I have left.

By sunrise the pale wolves have not come. Maybe the stranger wolf that visited me is alone too. Maybe she is just as afraid. How could she know that I would never hurt a lone wolf who came to me in peace? Not when my own sisters might be out there somewhere, just as lonely and frightened. I lift my head to look for her, but I am alone in a vast flat lake of grass.

The red has stopped running from the cut on my chest, and in place of the open slit is a long brown patch as rough as tree bark. It is stuck to my skin, and no amount of licking will move it. Thirst is making me whimper like a pup, but the instinct to hold still has me in a powerful grip. I lick the dew from the grass in the circle that I can reach without standing up. The paw that felt nothing before, now feels everything. Every little breeze that stirs my fur burns like a crackling fire. I lie still. The prairie is empty around me. Even the vulture has left.

In his place, packs of little birds visit me. They are small and grass-colored. They flit and sing, hopping from stalk to blade of grass, eating seeds and ants and watching the sky for hawks. When one comes, they scatter like smoke in the wind. All day I watch them, learning their voices, their smells, and the way they run through the sky. Some are all flap. Others flap and then hold, making one long swoop after another. My favorite is the green-backed hovering bird, the smallest of them all. A flash of purple shimmers at her throat. She has no pack, no muscle, no meat to her at all, but her flying puts every other bird to shame. The eagle, for all his power, is not so nimble. I watch her hover and dive until the wisps of clouds turn pink and gold.

By night the fire has gone from my foot, but hunger takes its place as chief among my pains. I eat grass.

In the morning my instinct to lie still is gone, but I have no strength to stand. If my pack were here, they would bring meat. I draw in air, as much as my body can hold, and call for their help. The

howl comes from deep inside of me. The high and low sounds roll up from my chest and out onto the wind. I turn my ears to each direction, straining to hear an answer.

No one howls back.

As the day goes on, one vulture and then another circles above me. A fat beetle scuttles by, and I lick it from the ground.

It is not so bad.

I have seen bears in a boulder field turning over rocks and eating the moths that live underneath. I creep forward and roll a small rock over. Nothing. And nothing under the next rock, but the next one I try has a bug. I eat it, and I am still hungry. I slap a butterfly out of the air with my good paw. I eat it, and I am still hungry. Another vulture joins the circle in the sky.

All creatures eat and all are eaten in the end, but I am not ready to be eaten, not today. I want my pack, my own pack. I want to run, to hunt, to live. I tell the vultures so as plainly as I can, but they keep circling above me. Waiting.

I cannot run. I can barely walk, but I can creep, and my nose tells me that mice are nearby. I take a step toward the smell, and rest, take another step, and rest. The sun is lower in the sky, and the green hovering bird comes again to dance around my head. When I turn back to the work at hand, what I had thought was a pile of stones in front of me uncoils and slithers away.

Mother warned me about snakes. They are

sharp-toothed and do not like to be stepped on. But are they food? Father would be ashamed of me for thinking so, but today, anything that moves is food. I crouch and prepare to stalk it, wondering how fast it can go. It makes a slow loop across the grass, and then like lightning it strikes, and with a wild squeak, an orange-brown vole disappears down its throat. And then the snake goes still, the vole inching down the snake's insides in a large speckled lump.

I kill the snake and gulp it down, vole and all. And then I snarl at the vultures in the sky.

"I will not die!" I growl. "Not today."

RAVEN

All the next day I sleep.

The stiff bark over my cut itches, but my tongue is too dry for licking. My leg hurts, but it will bear weight. In the cool of the night I walk toward the smell of water as slowly as a bear walks out of its winter den. At sunrise I see a ditch full of water ahead. The stench of cattle is thick on the ground, but I do not care. Without water I will die. A few steps closer, and the scent of men stops me in my tracks.

In the mountains we found the smell of men around circles of stones and ashes. It is the smell Mother taught me to fear above all others. Men are the worst of all dangers: unpredictable. Even bears, with all their seasonal moods, are easier to understand than men.

I duck low in the grass and watch. There is no sight or sound of men. I creep closer and get a look-smell at the prints. I am in no shape to fight or even run, but these prints have no toes, just a pad in back and another pad in front. Maybe this man cannot run either. Mother says they are fast for only having two legs, but they cannot fly like all of the other two-leggers. I cannot risk a fight, so I wait. Even though I am more thirsty than I have ever been. Even though the sun is rising, and with it the heat, and with that, my thirst. Still I wait and listen. And when I am sure, completely sure, that the men are gone, I dash for the water and plunge my head in.

Even with the stink of cattle, nothing in my life has ever tasted sweeter than that clear cold water. I drink until my belly is full. I find a hidden spot and doze all day long in the soft green grass. Mice come

to the water, and birds and rabbits. They are all too fast for me. By moonlight, a lumbering raccoon comes to drink. In one agonizing leap, I crush it. Pain shoots up my shoulder as I eat.

The next morning I am still lying in the grass and nibbling on the bones when a single raven swoops down and lands beside me. For a long time she regards me with her one-eyed stare. This raven is

black as dirt after a fire, just like all the rest, but she has a bare patch on her chest, picked clean of feathers. I look at it carefully. She looks at the brown bark on my chest just as carefully. What could have happened to her? She flies as well as I used to run. But why has she come to watch me so intently? I look at the bones around me. I have eaten every scrap. In my hunger, I left nothing for vultures or ravens or any other creature in need. Father would be ashamed of me. I sniff the skeleton and find a scrap of meat left on a leg bone. I nudge it toward the raven.

I remember how ravens talked to my father. How they led him to food and he thanked them with a gift of scraps. I need my pack, and maybe this raven can help me find them. I would give an entire elk to know what she can see from the air. I dip my head to her as I have seen birds do. She dips her head in return but does not take the meat. She circles around me, making a low rattling call.

I have seen a raven do this to an eagle that had caught a rabbit. The raven kept circling behind the eagle and pulling his tail feathers. A test. To attack the raven, the eagle would have had to let go of the rabbit. Except for wolves, nobody hunts as well as an eagle.

As I watched, I waited for the eagle to strike the raven dead. But even though the eagle towered over the raven, outweighed it, had far greater reach of wing, the eagle simply swallowed a few more bites of his kill and flew away.

At the time, it gave me hope in my quest to make Sharp lower his tail to me. The largest creature doesn't always win. Daring and persistence can triumph in the end. But now the raven's game makes me nervous. What could she want from me? I have given her all the meat I have left.

I get to my feet. The pain in my shoulder is less, but it feels stiff when I spin around to meet the raven face-to-face. She takes a few flaps backward and circles behind me again. I spin in the other direction. It isn't so stiff on that side. I shake out my matted fur and growl at her. She fluffs up her neck feathers and caws at me.

I should have asked Father how to speak to ravens. He seemed to understand them without words. The raven takes a scrap of bone in her beak and flies away. She climbs sharply, drops the bone directly over my head, and then dives for it. Against my will I crouch as she plummets toward me, and then, with a sharp *fwomp* of opening tail feathers, she catches the bone in her claws, pulls out of the dive, and circles me with chatters of victory.

A good trick.

She flies off ahead but, in my clear sight, drops the bone and dives for it again. This is no pup's game. Ravens do things for a reason. She is talking to me. She must know where to find meat. For all their savvy, ravens have the wrong beak for opening a hide. They need someone with teeth to get at the meat. I follow her, walking at first, but as my stiff leg loosens, I manage a slow trot.

She takes me out across the prairie, away from the water. There are countless game trails, each smell distracting me, but I cannot run fast enough to take down a coyote or a deer. One of the trails has a man smell. My father never hunted elk without checking for it. We walked away from easy pickings when the scent of men was on the ground. I am happy when the raven leads me away from that path.

The sun rises high in the sky, and I am weary enough to stumble when I hear the sound of rushing water. I stop-listen. There is no water smell. I can only smell hay and mint, and a few other things I have never smelled before. I pause and lift my head, turning from side to side to make sense of what my nose tells me. We come over a rise in the ground, and before me is a green meadow with no elk or deer or any other good thing in it, only nodding rows of dark green mint stretching on in unnatural straight lines.

Mother showed me a man's home ground once, from far away. It had plants in straight rows and great patches of bald earth.

"Men do things for no reason," she said.

A man sat upon a noise-making thing and rode its back around and around in wide circles over the dirt. For no reason. There was good water to one side of him and a deer with her fawn hiding in the dappled shade of an aspen on the other side of him. He had no use for food or water.

"Men do much with dirt," Mother said. "But they can kill with a look and a loud noise. Keep your distance. There is no understanding them."

The plants in rows make me anxious and I raise the fur on my shoulders to say so, but the raven coaxes me along. At least there is water in a ditch to drink. On the far side is a black river. A raven-black river. Completely still. Frozen in the heat of summer. The noisemakers of men go down this frozen black river faster than I can run. It smells like death. I am weary and disappointed. This is no place for a wolf. My family would never look for me here. I sit down and refuse to budge. The raven circles over my head and then swoops toward the shore of the black river. In my disgust I ignore her. The raven just as stubbornly swoops from me to the shore and back again. I do not care. I am not moving a step closer.

In all the shock of bad smells and loud noises, I almost don't hear the coyotes. They scamper around the mint field in a yapping yellow mass. They go to the raven and, with yelps of glee, fall upon whatever she has shown them. My stomach rumbles and water runs at my mouth. I have not eaten since yesterday. I need a full belly in order to heal as I should. I stand up and make my way toward the feeding coyotes. If they see I'm injured, they will turn on me. But if I can scare them away with a howl, I can carry off some meat. I warily circle downwind of them and then stand at the top of the ridge. I raise my head and let out my fiercest howl. The coyotes scatter as though they have been swept up by a storm. My tail rises to see them disappear

into the tall grass beyond the farm. I turn back to claim my prize.

It is small. Much of it is already gone. I am too hungry to complain, but then I see the paw. Not the broad hoof of an elk, nor the narrow one of deer. A paw. Five pads and four claws. What skin is left shows brown spots on white and soft drooping

ears. I turn away in disgust. I will be much hungrier than I am now before I stoop to take such leavings from a pack of witless coyotes. I turn and walk away.

As the sun lowers and the air cools I hear a howl, and for a moment hope leaps up in me. But it is only the bachelor wolves, just those two, and no family of mine. I ache from ears to tail. I want my pack. Still, any wolf is better than none. I turn toward their howling and lope away.

FOUND

The bachelor wolves are not hard to find. They howl on and on, a pride howl. They have taken meat. All the better for me. I will eat first and show them my hunting skill next time, when I am stronger. I am grateful. Under the rough bark that has grown over my wound, my muscles ache, and the hours of walking have made me weary.

I will have to beg to eat with them. I will hate lowering my tail to these fools, but I must start

somewhere. To join a pack you must fight your way in or beg, and I am in no shape for fighting. Warm had a way of creeping toward me to play-wrestle. He would let me win, and it made me love him and want to take care of him. I can pretend to be like Warm. I can make them want to take care of me.

I look to the mountains of my home ground, all lit up with a setting sun. The pale wolves will be there. They will be wet-marking over Mother's and Father's signposts, gathering in our meeting place, hunting our elk. Sharp will be one of them now. He is alive, at least. Would it be worth it to stay on the home ground and live among strangers? I could go back. I could beg my way into the enemy pack, and then at least I would be home. But what sort of a home would it be? Always following. Always eating last.

The bachelor wolves are not very impressive, but they are young. They will get better. I could lead them some day. I will make myself strong and fight my way to the top. The prairie has elk and streams of water to keep us alive, and the sight of the mountains to lift our heads at the end of the day. What more does a wolf need? With that thought I turn away from the mountains and head toward my new pack.

Twilight is the stillest time of day, and there is no wind to bring me the smell of what lies ahead. The bachelor wolves have stopped howling, but I can find them by the sound of their eating. They have caught something smaller than an elk. Smaller than a deer even. It has black-and-white skin. It must be the pup of a cow.

Father would not like that. Even worse than sheep, he would say. Only fit for coyotes and vultures, he would say. I am hungry. I have to eat what I can.

I stop a safe distance away and make plans. Even in the still air, the smell of fresh meat is so good it makes my stomach groan. I should wait until they have eaten the best parts so they will not mind sharing what's left. But if I wait too long, there will be nothing, and I am so hungry. It is too late in the day for birds to gather, so there is nobody to raise the alarm that I'm watching them. I sweep the tall grass all around to see if I have any competitors for the rest of the meat.

There is someone out there. I might have missed it, but a slight twitch in a thick clump of grass catches my eye. I turn my ears that way and raise my head to smell.

Warm? My heart skips a beat. I rise up taller and smell again.

It's him! My Warm! I would know him anywhere. I lift my head to howl, and then freeze.

He is hiding, hunched low to the ground, watching the bachelor wolves. His golden-gray fur blends with the pale green and silver grasses. He is alone and afraid. I am in no shape to defend him if the bachelor wolves attack. And they might. Warm and I together are more of a threat to them. I hold back my howl. I circle around silently and find a cluster of tall yellow flowers behind him. The bachelor wolves are still feeding. There is not enough wind to carry my smell to Warm. I roll a rock with my paw. He lifts his head and turns his ears my way.

"I'm here," I woof to him, as softly as I can.

A shiver goes through Warm. He turns around to look. I step into the open. He creeps toward me. I let my wag go. Warm! I knew he would follow me. When he is at last by my side, he rests his chin on my shoulder with a deep sigh. Whatever happens now, we will be together.

"You're here," Warm says. "I dreamed that you would be here."

I rub my chin against his neck. "We will travel

together," I say. "Just like we planned." I can face anything now.

"The prairie is not so bad," I begin. "There are elk. Lots of them. And water. We will find a way. Just the two of us."

I nose him from shoulder to—

And then I see them. Claw marks. From his back to his rump. Long, red, and angry. His back legs tremble even when he is standing still. I do not know how he is standing at all. The pain that still burns my shoulder must be nothing compared to his. His wounds are not running with red. Not now. But they cut clear through his fur and skin and deep into muscle.

I feel a revenge growl deep in my throat. Who did this? I will tear them apart with my own teeth! But even as my growl builds to a snarl, I know that whoever did this was bigger and stronger than me. How will I protect Warm now? I am wounded and weak myself. He is thin. So thin. I can feel each rib under my tongue as I lick his wounds.

"Rest," I say to him. "I will bring you meat." I nose him down where the tall grass covers us both. He needs rest. And food. He needs me.

"I knew you would get away," Warm says as he curls up on the ground at my feet. "You are the fastest of us all."

I lick his ears the way he likes. "Across enemy ground, and clear out here on the flat, you never gave up."

"I would follow you anywhere," he says.

My heart aches for him. He has not said what became of Mother and the pups. I want to know the truth, and I dread knowing. I have often seen Warm scared but never this weak. I cannot ask him. Not now. I will feed him. I will make him better. And then if Mother and the pups survived, we will find them together. I turn back toward the bachelor wolves and their kill. Toward the food that will save us both.

LIGHTNING

In my determination to take care of Warm, I almost miss the man smell.

I crouch-freeze.

Men are walking toward the bachelor wolves, slowly and quietly. The wolves are so busy at their meat, still struggling over which one is the lead wolf, they do not hear the men coming. Their noses are so full of their kill, they do not smell the men coming. The men crouch on the ground on a rise just above them.

Mother's words come to mind. "They can kill with a look and a loud noise."

I watch and wait. The men lift black sticks to their shoulders. Something is bad here. I can feel it. The fur all over my body rises.

"Hold still," I say to Warm.

He lies motionless. The bachelor wolves have not caught scent of the men or me. They are busy with their food. The smell of it is agony. I need that meat. Warm needs it even more. If only the men would go away, I would be begging for my portion, eating, bringing a bellyful to share with Warm. I am tempted, sorely tempted, to join the feast. The men are just watching.

But Mother's words linger. "They can kill with a look."

What does that mean?

And then the men throw lightning from their sticks. A flash of fire, a clap of thunder, and the wolves go down. The brown wolf goes to the ground without even a cry. The gray one yelps aloud. He struggles to run, but his back legs won't move. He drags them for a few agonizing steps. And then another lightning bolt flares, and another. The men are shouting now. Both wolves are down, but the lightning and thunder go on. Each burst makes the dead bodies jump.

The sound of it shatters my heart. Panic floods me and my breath comes in gasps, as if I am drowning.

"Run!"

Warm is already moving. Rigid with fear, he runs stiff-legged, as fast as his wounds will let him. I bound after him. Mother taught us to scatter when the scent of a hunting cougar is on the ground, but I cannot leave Warm now. We run. Flat out. Shoulder to shoulder. I will save him. He is all I have.

A shout comes from behind. The thunder stops.

"Don't. Leave me," Warm pants by my side.

Fear drives me to familiar ground. Back over the path of the raven from this morning. I search my memory for some scrap of cover along the way. Some place. Any place. The mountains had trees and ravines, thickets and caves. On the prairie, there is only room to run and nowhere to hide. But if we can run far enough, darkness will hide us, and the useless noses of men will never lead them to us.

"A little farther," I say to Warm as he stumbles beside me. "Just a little more."

There is a tree. A hawthorn. We turn toward it, crouching underneath its spiny branches. Warm drops his head to the ground, breathing hard. I cannot see his wounds in the dark, but I can smell that red has begun to seep out of them. I curl my body around him and put all my hope in silence.

There is a crack like a stick being broken, and a light shines out from where the men stand. It is as if a star has come out of the sky. An icicle of light sweeps across the grass. I hold my breath. It passes over us. I can feel Warm tremble with fear. The star swings back and shines all its light on us. The dark green leaves and black hawthorn berries glisten in the light. The light does not move on. It stays, and we are frozen in its icy touch.

The growl of a noisemaker breaks the silence. Warm whimpers in terror. I shush him with a look. They will get inside the noisemaker and go away, like men do. Then a second growl follows the first. They will go. They will get in their noisemakers, and we will never smell them again.

The ground shivers as the noisemakers begin to move. They pick up speed, and I can feel-hear-smell that they are coming. I want to run. I need to hide. Pain saps my courage. There is nowhere else to go. I can feel Warm's heart against my chest, pounding as wildly as my own.

The noisemakers slow, and then stop. The cold white light fills me with dread even though I am still hidden in shadow.

A clap of thunder—a flash of lightning!

I feel-smell the sharp tooth of something whiz past my ears. We leap up, scampering away from the light that now swings back and forth across the grass. The lightning comes again in bursts. Again I feel it scorch the air above my head. A tooth falls dead in front of me, kicking up a puff of dust.

Warm swerves to the side and I dodge the opposite way. The light cannot follow us both. I will draw it away from him. I yelp to attract attention. I make noise as I sprint, while Warm runs in complete silence, with all the strength he has left. The light swings toward me and away, as lightning snaps at my feet. Warm cries out: one sharp wail drowned out by lightning. My heart is bursting. I cannot see Warm. I can only run and hope.

The mint field lies ahead, and I plunge into it. The thick stalks and leaves brush against me, burying all smell of everything else. I will find Warm on the other side. I burst out of the field, and the black river lies ahead. I can still hear the lightning behind me over the roar of noisemakers coming down the black river. I am too frightened to stop. Too desperate to be afraid. I do not break my stride. The black river is hard and sticky at the same time. The heat of the day lingers on it. A huge noisemaker lets out a call like a bull elk. It swerves to one side and the other. I jump for the far shore and it whooshes behind me. The far side of the black river is steep and grassy and dark. I fall down it, rolling over and over, tucking in my legs so they will not break. I tumble down in darkness, and when I finally skid to a stop, the night has gone silent, and I am utterly alone.

At first I can only lie flat on the steep rocky hillside. The ground still seems to be spinning. My breath comes in ragged gasps. My own heart beating is the only sound I can hear. When my ears stop ringing, when the dazzle of lightning fades and I can see again in the dark, I look for Warm. Listen for him. Long for him. But he does not come.

The thunder and lightning have stopped. The sweep of cold light across the ground is gone. The sound of the noisemakers is gone. And Warm. Warm is gone.

I should go back. If he is alive, he will need me. I look up the long dark slope. I shudder at the memory of the noisemaker whizzing by at my heels. The sticky feel of the black river—the bitter smell. I never want to cross it again.

I should go back. But the dread of all I have seen-heard-smelled—how could anyone survive it?

I cannot face the men, the lightning, the noisemakers again. I pick myself up off the ground. Everything hurts. I look over my shoulder. There is nothing but death behind me. Nowhere to go but onward.

I hear water below me. There's not a tree or a shrub, not even tall grass to hide me. I pick my way around rocks, test my footing on loose stones. The sound of water at the canyon floor guides me in the dark. I want nothing except a place to hide. Somewhere secret and safe where men will never find me. I want it more than meat and water and the light of day. I limp down and down and farther down. Rocks give way to grass and then shrubs and finally trees. By nose and instinct I find a hidden spot along the canyon bottom with a rocky ledge overhead and a pine tree with branches that sweep the ground in front to hide me from . . . everything. I turn in a weary circle, whispering the names of my pack for comfort. I am asleep before I hit the ground.

In my dreams I am running in panic through a thunderstorm that never ends. I wake when the sun finally reaches deep into the canyon. Everything still hurts, and I am too exhausted to take a few steps to water. I sniff the air for danger. I smell again for hope. I fall asleep again, thirsty and listening. I wake the next day, with more thirst and with no hope at all for Warm—he was weak and wounded before the lightning came. I lie listening a long time before I risk a drink. The next morning I risk a longer drink. I am not so stiff as before. The bruises from my fall are slowly fading. But the hard edges of my memory become sharper. They push deep into me like a tooth.

Warm followed me. He found me. I promised to protect him. Promised.

I remember all those summer days in the mountains when Warm let me play-hunt him, helped me get stronger, sharpened my stalk and my spring. All those times when he pushed me to run faster. All those times when he took the nips and snaps from

Sharp and Pounce so I would not have to take them. He made me the wolf I am. And I lost him. I was not strong enough, not fast enough to save his life.

He died alone, with no one beside him to sing his name to the wolf star.

In my dreams I can hear Warm and smell him. I run and run and run and just when I have almost found him running far ahead of me, I wake up, weary and heartsick. The skin over my belly grows slack, but I do not feel hunger. I only feel empty.

CANYON

Another day passes and another and then my hunger wakes up before I do. I must stand up and live, or lie down and die. I step out of my hiding spot and shake out my fur in the sun. I stretch back legs and front. My wounded shoulder is better. I wade along the rocky edge of the stream. The uneven ground that was agony to walk on before is not so bad now. I look-smell for some sign of deer or elk that water here. My heart sinks even as I do. The whole time I lay hidden, nothing came to drink. The canyon walls are too steep and the shore too rocky. I can feel the loose skin of my belly sway as I walk. Far above the canyon walls, I see the silhouette of a raven. I bark a call just because it has been so long since I had anyone to talk to.

The raven calls back! She circles down and lands beside me. She has the same bare patch on her chest as my raven from before. My raven! She struts the length of me, and I stand tall to show that I am stronger than when we first met.

The rattling call of a kingfisher makes both of us jump. It flies low over the stream. It keeps saying the same thing. Over and over. Loudly. It hovers, like the tiny green bird on the prairie did. Then it dives into the water and emerges with a fish.

Good trick.

I am hungry.

Just as I am considering what a wolf could do to persuade a bird to give up her kill, my raven takes off, circling upward. She swoops down the stream. She is twice the kingfisher's size. She knocks it sideways and it drops the fish. The raven dives, quick as a darting dragonfly, and snatches the fish before it hits the water.

Great trick!

I am so hungry.

My raven lands by my side and makes an offer to share her food. But the fish is small. I move down to a quiet pool where I do not have to hear her and the kingfisher yell at each other over less than a mouthful of fish.

I drink. There is something in the water. Something big. I cannot smell it, but I can see it moving, speckled blue against the speckled gray stones in the stream. I have seen bears do the trick of pulling fish out of a stream. I crouch-stare at the water. I do not know how deep the water is. I only know that I am hungry.

A bear can lift a fish from water with one slap. I give it a try, but the water is too deep. The fish makes a dash for cover. I jump in, jaws open and hopes high. Three bites come up empty, and then I have him! Water fills my nose and ears, and I scramble blindly for the shore.

Water streams from my fur. The fish is bendy in the middle. It flops in my mouth like no elk or deer or proper food would. Father would turn his back to me if he saw me like this. Sharp would laugh. But I am hungry, and they are not here to help me

hunt. I drop-bite, drop-bite, drop-bite the fish on the rocks, and in time it holds still.

A fish is crispy outside and squashy inside. The bones are so small they tickle going down. It does not taste like food, but it fills me up just the same. My raven is happy to eat the head and tail. I wash the odd taste from my mouth and take my fill of water. The raven flies downstream, away from all I have ever known. Here between the canyon walls, I cannot see my home ground or smell it or hear the sounds I have grown up with. Even so, I can feel the mountains tug at me. They turn me around. But there is no one to go home to. My raven circles back, swoops round my shoulders, brushing my fur with her wing tips. She alights on a pine branch, tilts her head to the side, chatters to me, and then flies downstream.

My father followed ravens. I turn away from my home ground and go where she leads me.

We travel along together, leaving the black river and the cruelty of men far behind. We look for springs and trickles and pools of water where I can hunt what comes to drink. My raven is always at my shoulder, ready to share the meat I have opened, whether it is fish or rabbits or stripe-tailed raccoons.

Everything here is different—the smell of the wind, the color of the dirt. I look-smell for elk, but there are none. I listen for the howls of a pack that might take me in, but at sundown I only hear the thin voices of crickets and toads. When I turn to search the horizon for my home ground, I cannot even see the mountains. I know where they should be, but I cannot see them.

This open land has nothing to break it, no trees, no rivers, and no border marks of wolves. Everywhere I look, it smells the same. The ground is not completely flat. There are bumps. Gullies. Slowly rising land with stripes of rusty- and sandy-colored dirt, gently falling land with more streaks of black, brown, and red. The wind is so dry the skin of my nose cracks.

I grow stronger every day—stronger in my body.

But the farther I get from the mountains, the harder it is to hold up my tail. There is no one here to care for and wrestle with and share smells with. No one to sing with. No tails to catch. No ears to nip. No one to sit shoulder to shoulder with and watch the wolf star as it rises before the sun. Even a summer night is cold when you sleep alone.

ALMOST

After many days of walk-trot-eat-rest, we find something completely new. My raven, flying ahead as usual, appears to sit down in midair. Not soaring on rising air. Not hovering. Sitting. In the middle of the air!

I approach slowly. A raven has her tricks. But as I get closer I see she is sitting on a thin gray line. It runs straight like the rows of the mint field, straight like the black river. It must be a man thing. I crouch-growl-sniff. There is only a faint, long-ago scent of men. I listen in every direction. Nothing. The air is still and the shadows are short.

I come to the gray lines watchfully.

My raven pokes at her feathers. Shakes out her wings. There is no fear in her. I come closer. There are three lines of gray—low, middle, and high. Branches grow through the lines and stick into the ground. It is the oddest man thing yet. The lines catch tumbleweeds. They make a roosting spot for birds. What man would need that? There is no understanding them. When I lean against the lines, they lean but do not fall. No matter. It is easy to jump over them.

I am ready to move on when I catch a whiff of something familiar. I follow the lines until I find tufts of white sheep-covering. I do not need such coyote food. We ate a rabbit yesterday, and if I can find water I might take a deer while it is drinking. But there is another smell in with the sheep, a better smell. I nose along the lines until I find a tuft of fur. It is white, but not so fluffy as sheep-covering. It is true fur, too long and too pale for deer or elk, wrong smell for fox or coyote. It is not a wolf smell. But it is a wolflike smell. I have been so long away from my family, I throw back my head and howl.

An answer comes, carried on the wind. It is not a howl. Not a coyote's high-pitched yip. It is a deep voice and strange to my ear.

"Oof, oof."

I answer without thinking.

"Here I am! Who are you?"

"Oof, oof, ooo!" the almost-wolf calls back.

I cannot quite catch the meaning.

I call again. My tail is high in the air and wagging like a pup. I swivel my ears to pinpoint the sound.

"Aoof!" the almost-wolf says.

I do not care what that means. I take off running. As I draw closer, the smell becomes stronger. The confusing, almost-wolf smell of it drives me wild. If only it were not mixed in with sheep smells, I could remember if I have smelled it before.

As I draw closer, the sheep smells grow stronger too. That could mean trouble. I slow down to make my run silent and pick my approach so the wind will not carry news of me.

Ahead is a barn. My raven gives a warning caw. A noisemaker is sleeping beside the barn. I look-sniff for the source of the woofs. It is a she. I am nearly certain. If only there were not so many other smells to confuse me. The man smell grows as I get closer to the barn. If there is a wolf here, or an almost-wolf, I should warn her. I should take her far away, where she will be safe. Behind the barn are rows of gray lines. The almost-wolf is inside the lines with a big pack of mother sheep and their pups. The almost-wolf is looking right at me, whimpering and wagging.

A man pup is inside the gray lines with her. It is touching the almost-wolf. It is stroking her beautiful fur gently around the ears where Mother used to lick me. It is not killing the almost-wolf, not even trying. The man pup does not have a lightning stick.

There must be some trick. It looks my way, but it does not see me in the yellow and gray of the tall grass and rocky ground. Its tiny nose does not catch my scent. The mother sheep know I am here. They gather their pups under them and move as

far from me as the gray lines will let them go.

The almost-wolf knows I am near too.

"Oof, oof, ooo!"

She tries to howl. She lowers her tail to ask me to come closer. She woofs and wags, circles away from the gray lines and back to them. She doesn't know any wolf words, not yet, but her body says come

closer. It has been so long since I've had someone to speak with, to wrestle with, to run alongside. Far too long since I have had the company of another living thing curled up with me in the cold of night. She is oddly marked with white and sandy-brown patches. I call to her again. The man pup jabbers like a jay to the almost-wolf. It strokes her fur and she does not flinch. I want to stroke that fur too. I want the sound of her, the smell of her, the company of her on my travels.

"Come away with me. Jump the lines."

She throws back her head and copies my howl.

But she does not seem to know the meaning.

"Jump. It's not too high. You can do it!"

She copies my howl with no more understanding. The man pup pulls her away from the lines, and she obeys it. It is small. She could break away from its grasp with no effort at all. She could crush its bones in one bite. But she stays.

"Follow me!" I call.

I beat my front feet to the ground, laying out scent for her to follow. She wants to come. I see it in her wag, but she won't jump the lines.

And then the barn door opens. My raven takes off, flying low and fast. A full-size man comes out. It has a lightning stick. I am filled with horror. It calls to the almost-wolf and she goes to it, right up to it, lightning stick and all! I do not understand her. I want to call her away one last time, but it is not worth my life. I swallow my howl and all my loneliness with it and creep away. My scent is on the ground for the almost-wolf to follow if she ever gains the courage. But for now, I am on my own, and come nightfall even the moon is gone.

FOOD

The thought of the man and his lightning stick haunts me as I run. Even the raven's company is little comfort. Dread and bitter memories push me onward. My feet fall into a rhythm, but the memory of the almost-wolf won't let me go. I stop. I look back. She could have jumped that fence. Could have come when I called her. But she let the man pup touch her. She lives surrounded by man smell. Maybe she learned their ways like the bachelor wolves learned the ways of the coyote. I am better off on my own, but I want her company just the same.

In worrying over her, I miss my chance at getting a rabbit. My raven scolds me as she swoops circles around my head. I snarl at her even though I know she is right. When you only eat little things, you have to catch something every day. I keep up my pace, but sharpen my eye so I will not miss the next meal.

The land is drier now. Not a tree in sight, and all I can smell is dust and cowpats. The slack skin over my belly reminds me of how long it has been since I ate deer and elk. Come sundown, my raven finds a roost, but I keep looking for food. Nothing comes by, not raccoons, not foxes, not even mice. I flop down beside the shrub where my raven is roosting and try to ignore my growling stomach.

In the morning I wait for my raven to scout for a meal. She flies in a broad circle and comes back. Nothing to report. She takes off again. I wait. A fat juicy beetle waddles by right under my nose.

I am never. Never. Going to eat bugs again.

I stand up and stretch. I search

the sky for my raven. The heat of the day comes up, and I am in the only shade I can see. I stay, and my hunger grows with the rising heat. The only living things I see are geese high overhead, and even they, with all their empty-headed honking, know better than to land here. The shadows grow long before the raven is back. She comes flying low and straight to me. She is glad of something. She circles me twice. Lands at my feet and bobs her head to me.

It must be food, food she can't open if she came all this way back for me. I take off at a run and she leads the way. Hunger nibbles away at my speed. My raven circles back twice for me to catch up. But then when the sun goes down, she finds a shrub and just puts her head under her wing as if the dark makes a difference. Who cares that the moon is gone? There is starlight. And nothing but dirt and cowpats to worry about here on the flat ground. I growl at my raven. She puffs up her feathers and caws in protest. Fine. I will find the meat she was taking me to on my own.

There are no circling vultures in the sky to show where the meat is. My stomach is groaning. I lift up my head and complain to the stars.

Nobody answers me.

I go back to my raven and lie down under her roost, and even in my dreams I am hungry.

My raven and I are up and running at first light. Dry ground rolls by under my paws. I watch my raven, flying ahead, as hungry as me. The pain in my shoulder is gone and only the pain of hunger drives me on. The ground begins to rise, and above me I can hear-smell the black river before I see it. I woof a warning to the raven, but she has no caution. She circles back and then urges me on. I go more slowly now, look-listening for men, breathing in the foul air that hangs in a cloud over the black river. But the raven is still urging me on. I follow her along the bank even as noisemakers whoosh by.

There is a dead deer on the shore of the black

river. My raven lands on the hide, hopping for joy. It is a full-grown buck with meat enough to feed a pack. The hunger I have felt for days and days, ever since I ran from the mountains, roars up in me, and I am wild with it. I forget my sorrows, my loneliness, everything. I sink my teeth into the hide. I open the belly. There is no one to snatch the best bits out of my mouth. No one to make me watch while they eat all the richest meat. I take the whole liver and all the heart, feeling stronger with every bite. I strip skin and gulp muscle. Red runs down my chin. My belly fills until my skin is stretched tight. There is still meat left. It smells so good, I want to roll in it. I am full and keep eating. The sun goes down and I eat still more. Finally, at last, when my hunger is gone and my fear of hunger gone with it, I look up.

Only then do I see my raven eating beside me and hear the noisemakers still rushing by. Only then do I remember that my home is downstream and on the far side of this black river. Only then do I take a good look at the deer I have been eating. It is a full-grown buck with many prongs on his antlers. I always save the bones and their rich, savory centers for last. As I nose among the bones, I see that something is very wrong. Every rib is broken. Not one cracked bone, as happens in a fall. All the bones are shattered, as if a huge boulder fell on the deer. There is no boulder beside the body and no cliff for one to fall from. This is a blow like nothing I have ever seen. Even the

largest bear could not crush a deer like this.

Curious now, I paw through the skin, looking for the tooth marks of the creature that killed this deer. If there is some new animal, something bigger and more dangerous than anything I know, I must learn all I can about it. I find no puncture in the usual spot on the neck. Nothing in the back of the head like a cougar strike. No bite mark around the lower leg like coyotes make. But in the skin of the belly there are chips of ice. But this ice is warm to the touch and sharper than a bobcat's claw. There are a few more pieces of not-ice on the ground and even more on the bank. I have been ignoring the sound and stench of the black river, but now I watch as a noisemaker goes by. It shakes the ground as it comes. It is so fast it makes a breeze in the still night air. I look at my raven and back at the trail of not-ice. My raven bows her head to me, as if to confirm what I fear.

A noisemaker did this. Crushed this deer in mid-gallop and kept going without stopping to eat or even give a nod of thanks to the life that sustains all who run on four paws. Mother was right. There is no understanding men. I shudder at the thought that I ever set a foot on the black river. I will never cross it again. My mountains are somewhere on the far shore, but I will never go home.

I lift my head and call out to my lost family. I know they cannot hear me. Maybe none of them are left. Still I call to them.

"I am here. I survived."

No one answers. I drop my head, weary with sorrow. The raven leads me away from the black river. I stumble after her to a cluster of birches and drop to the ground against their pale smooth trunks. The raven speaks to me in a soft voice, but before I can work out what she has said, I lay down my head and dream of the mountains.

FEAR

I sleep all through the night and long past sunrise. A full belly keeps me drowsy all day long. I should be happy, but I am haunted by memories. After a hunt there was always joy in the pack. Howling. Wrestling. Games of chase. And when the celebrating was done, we would all lie down together, paws and tails overlapping, the comforting scent of my pack all around me. Sometimes I would keep myself awake just to hear the sound of them breathing.

"All is well," Mother would murmur to me. "We are together."

There is more food to eat. I should go back to the

deer. But the thought of eating alone makes my tail droop clear down to the ground. When I finally stir myself, the moon is a pale yellow claw on the horizon and my raven is head under wing in the trees above me. I shake from nose to tail. I square my shoulders and beat my front paws to the ground to test my strength. I growl as though I am a lead wolf. But there is no one to hear me. No one to share my food. No one to curl up with and rest. The pain of my injuries, the pain of hunger, is nothing compared to the pain that stills my wag and holds in my howl.

Though I hate it, I go to the shore of the black river one last time. I call out one last goodbye to my lost family. No one will hear me. I can barely hear myself, but I give them one last howl. It is all I have. As I turn to go, a noisemaker rounds the bend. Its fires throw a sweep of light across the far bank. In that light, just for a moment, I see a flash of amber. My heart skips a beat.

It is a wolf.

Another noisemaker, another sweep of light, and

I can see black ears and a dark face with shining amber eyes.

A wolf—a true wolf!

I yip-spin like a pup. I call to her. I breathe in the smells, searching for a scent of her. The smells of the black river nearly choke me but underneath them, yes, a female wolf.

I yip-spin again and call her over. She does not answer, but in the flashes of light that fall across her I can tell that she sees me. She paces the far bank, strong and black and beautiful. She is young like me. A perfect hunting partner. Already I can feel her running shoulder to shoulder beside me. Already I can imagine licking her ears. How can I get her to cross?

Food! Obviously food. I dash over to yesterday's deer. I sink my teeth into the meatiest leg and tug it free.

A sweep of light from a noisemaker swings across the shattered rib bones. I drop the leg in horror. The black river. It will kill her. I scramble

back. The ground is trembling with the approach of the longest noisemaker I have ever seen.

"Danger! Stay away!" I call to her.

She lifts her head to howl, but as she does, the long noisemaker makes the death cry of a bull elk. It rings in my ears, drowning out the stranger wolf's voice. The rumble of it makes the little stones on the shore hop. The whoosh of air pushes me back a step. When my ears stop echoing and my eyes clear from the dazzle of light, the black wolf is still there, pacing the far shore.

"Do not cross!" I howl.

Already another noisemaker is on the way. She

runs up the bank and then turns just in time.

"Stay back!" I call to her.

Even as I say it, I am stabbed with regret. I want her company here on the far shore where nothing but strange ground lies before me. She does not back away from the noisemakers, and I love her courage, even as I am filled with horror at what might happen if she tries to cross.

She calls to me, but her voice is drowned out. She tries again with a running start. I cannot bear to watch, but I cannot turn away. At the last minute she shies away from the approaching noisemaker. I gasp with relief, but no sooner does the thing pass than she tries again. She is stubborn. More like Pounce than Warm. How can I persuade her to stay away when she can't hear my warning?

"Do not die," I whisper. I cannot bear it—not after Father—not after Warm. I have had too much of death. I will not watch another. I lift up my head and howl a long "*NOOOOOOO.*"

My raven hears me. She braves the darkness to fly to my side, and something in her unblinking gaze reminds me of Growl. Growl had a look, a face he made, if we pups were about to stray out of bounds. If we got more than a moment's dash from the safe cover of our den, he would raise the fur on his shoulders and beat the ground with his front paws. He would dip his head low, glare us straight in the eye, and make a low sucking growl. I could not look away from that look. It terrified me. He did not lay a tooth or paw on us, but we never—never ever—crossed the boundary he set for us.

Do all wolves do this? I have to try.

I think about how Growl looked at me when I was about to cross a line. I move directly across the black river from the black wolf. I put my body in the pose of an angry pup-watcher. I wait for the light from a noisemaker to wash over me, and I give her my fiercest pup-watcher growl. I know she cannot hear me, but she can see the way I stand and beat the ground and lower my head. She can see me watch her with that commanding look, my lips curled back with growling.

"Do not pass!"

I put all my fear and loneliness into that growl. I glare at her with all the protective menace I can muster.

"Do not pass! Do not pass!"

I beat the ground until my shoulders ache and my voice is raw. When I can

do nothing more, I pace the bank of the black river and search for her amber eyes. Only darkness looks back at me. I stumble away from the shore, my growl worn away to a whimper.

I did it. I saved her.

WATER

My raven finds me in the dark. She perches on the ground beside me all night long. When the sun rises, I follow her lead. She is all the pack I have now. We leave the black river far behind, and I am grateful. It is quiet on the flat ground, and windy. It will be many days before I am hungry again, but by the time the sun is beating down on me with the full strength of midday, I am thirsty. The rocks get sharper as we travel. I slow to a trot and pick my way around them. I look-smell for water, but there is no trace.

I flop down under a shrub. Its shade is no bigger

than my body. It is not any cooler underneath, but the shimmer of sun has made my eyes weary. I close them to rest, panting away the heat. My mouth is dry as an old bone, and still there is no scent of water. Ants crawl up in my fur, and I don't have the energy to shake them off. My raven circles back and waits in the tree. She is eager to keep going. The sky is an easy run. No stones to bruise her feet. She calls to me.

"Wait!" I bark back. "Dark is coming. Cooler air is coming."

I say my reasons as patiently as a wolf can, but my raven is not persuaded. She flies off again. I follow her, but slowly.

The heat of the day passes, and we have not found water, but my raven holds to the sunset line as if she has flown this way before and knows where water lives. We pass more of the gray lines, but these are rusty and lying on the ground or wound up in a tangled ball. The smell of men is long gone, but I refuse to go near them. Far away on the horizon I see cows, rust colored against the silver and gold of grass and sagebrush. I am not hungry. Thirst is all I can think of. I am sure my raven will lead us to water. She needs it as much as I do. When the sun goes down, she finds her tree for the night.

"Where is the water?" I growl.

She turns her back to me.

"I followed you and there's no water!"

She only caws back, shakes out her wings, and settles in to sleep.

I find a stand of junipers and lie down to rest my sore paws. I imagine wading into the ice-cold streams of my home ground. Sleep does not come. The ground is rocky. The wind is hot and dry. Nothing smells like home. I whimper like a pup and don't even care if my raven hears me.

In my desperate thirst, I remember that under the hard bark of the cut on my chest, my own body ran with red. I would drink even that. I lick at the bark to open my skin. It is rough and my tongue is drier than sand, but the edges of the bark lift up.

I lick harder. It stings, but I don't care. The edges crumble away, and then at last the whole strip of the bark breaks free. With a grateful gasp I lick at my chest, but there is no red to drink—only a smooth white mark where the cut once was.

I throw back my head and howl and howl and howl until I have howled up the moon. In its light I close my eyes at last and fall asleep. The moon carries me in a dream all the way back to my home ground and all its falling waters: sweet, clear, and cold.

When I wake I am even more thirsty. The grit of dirt and sand in my fur itches as much as the bugs. No amount of rolling and scratching makes it better. Birds fly overhead, rivers of them. They fly away from the sunrise, songbirds and packs of quacking ducks and geese in their long lines. My raven takes off and follows them, but I am too angry, too footsore, too thirsty to follow. I lie back down under the juniper.

Birds keep coming. A cloud of speckled songbirds swoop and dive as if they are one creature. A pack of giant gray cranes, loud and long necked, follow them. They fly in the same direction, talking all at once, but lowering to the ground as they go.

Maybe all the birds are on to something. I get up, clamber on top of a boulder, and take a look. On the horizon is a stripe of green and a shimmer of blue beyond it.

I take off running, long strides pounding the ground, the sore pads of my feet forgotten. All I can think about is water. I run so fast I flush out a family of owls from their nest. A long-eared rabbit scatters in one direction and his mate in another. The ground softens as I get closer. I can smell green growing things and a lake full of water.

I crash into the lake and drink. The water is cool and still and tart. I drink it in gulps, panting with relief. The mud soothes my feet after so many days on rocky ground. I roll over and over, drowning all the itchy bugs in my fur. I kick up water just for the pleasure of hearing it splash. Full at last, I wade to the shore and shake. And then I duck under the water and shake again, just because I can.

There are more birds around the lake than I have ever seen in my life. The huge gray cranes that flew in ahead of me are still making a racket. They flap their broad wings and jump-spin like pups fresh out of the den. There are smaller cranes with long yellow legs. Pure-white swans with long necks and

black bills bow to one another. Ducks and geese of every color swim in circles; some of them carry their pups on their backs. Others have pups trailing after them in a line of fluff and quacks. If a wolf didn't mind feathers, he could eat his fill.

The warm wind dries my fur, and I look to the shoreline for a meal. Things with hooves come to the water at dusk. I will be ready for them when they do.

I pick a spot where there are many hoofprints in

the mud. I settle in the tall grass nearby and wait. As the shadows grow long, a yearling buck comes to the water. His horns are short, and there are no scars on him as tested bucks have. He is wary, but not wary enough. I spring on him and land the killing blow before he has time to run. He falls at the water's edge.

I pause for a moment before eating. A moment of respect, as Father taught me. This is the first kill I have taken on my own. The little things—fish, snakes, raccoons, and mice—were nothing to celebrate. But this kill—Father would be proud of this.

My raven will be hungry. We have not eaten in days. I call her and open the hide. Good things spill out in a warm steamy pile. I take a few bites and call for my raven again. She led me to water all the way across the dry flats. I will be glad of her company over the meat. It feels wrong to eat alone.

My raven doesn't come.

I call her again.

A whole pack of ravens rises up from the grass

with a great rattling call. They come to me. They swarm around the meat. I am happy to share. I take the parts that are a wolf's due and settle in to chewing as the ravens pick over their bits of meat.

I search for mine among them, but they look all alike. I call to her, but none of them look up. I sniff the air, but ravens all smell the same to me. My raven had a bald patch on her chest much like the white line on my shoulder. I look for it, and when I find her, I yip a greeting.

She carries on eating and squabbling with her pack as if I am not there. As if kinship between a wolf and a raven is impossible. As if all the days we have traveled together mean nothing at all. When the shadows grow long and the air cools, every one of the ravens takes to the sky without a backward look. They roost together on the other side of the water, far away from me. My raven has her pack now.

I have eaten my fill. There is more water than I can drink, and yet I have never felt so empty. I know,

I have always known, that the raven could never be a pack mate to me. No mere bird could take the place of Pounce or Wag—certainly not of Warm. And yet we have taken a journey together. We have shared meat. She was my guide and companion. The soft talk of doves and the beauty of the setting sun do not comfort me.

MOUNTAIN

I turn away from my only friend and walk on along the lakeshore. The cool mud is soft under my feet. I search for the tracks of a wolf among all the duck and deer and coyote prints. There is plenty of everything here—except the one thing I want more than water and food. There is no sign that any wolf has passed this way. There are more things to eat than I can name, and nobody to eat them with.

Still, I cannot be downcast with a full belly and a star-speckled sky. I have missed traveling by night. Missed the chill of the mountains. I have been thirsty for clouds and mists and rain. Here on the flat ground, even the moonlight is relentless.

The ground around me stretches out in every direction. It all looks exactly the same. I pause and taste the wind. Lake water and birds are to one side of me, and nothing but sagebrush everywhere else. The rat-a-tat call of the frogs in the lake makes me shudder. I tried a frog once because Sharp dared me to do it. It was the worst thing I have ever eaten, all slime on the outside and bitter in the middle. Even Wag, who once dug up a hornets' nest, knew better than to eat frogs. Pounce mocked me for days. I am never going to eat anything with spots ever again.

Where in all of this land would wolves live? There is food aplenty, but nothing feels like home to me. I turn away from the water. By the time the sun comes up, the lake is a silver-blue shimmer far behind me, and a mountain lies on the horizon. It's a single mountain, but I am drawn to it anyway. Elk like a sloping meadow. If there is a wolf anywhere, it will be on a mountain. I move faster now that I can see my footing clearly. Rising ground and crisp air are welcome changes.

There are a few thin stripes of snow reaching down from the peak, so I know there will be water above me. I climb at a steady pace. The pale green clumps of sagebrush give way to darker green junipers. The trees are few and far apart here, and smaller than the ones I knew when I was growing up. They aren't hiding anything good to eat. I can smell marmots from somewhere in the cliffs and boulder fields ahead of me. They have the good sense to hold so still that I cannot see them, unlike the ground squirrels, who have no sense of any kind and dash out of cover without even looking for danger. They are not worth the trouble of hunting. A mouthful of stripes and a squeak, that's all you get. Even bears, who eat everything under the sun, including moths, hardly bother with a ground squirrel.

As I climb, trees give way to open meadows with every kind of flower in the world. I zigzag all across the green-yellow-orange-blue of it and tell myself I'm looking for some sign of deer or elk to eat, but I'm still full from yesterday. What I really want is a scent or track or tuft of hair from another wolf.

This is a mountain. A mountain! There should be wolves.

I have run for days and days. The moon has gone from fat to thin and is growing fatter again. Ever since I crossed the black river, I have not seen a single wolf scat. No paw prints. No scent marks. I had brothers and sisters, a whole pack. I never imagined that the world could be so big or that I could be so alone in it. I remember the wolf on the shore of the black river. The one I drove away. I am not sorry that I saved her from being crushed by noisemakers. I want her to live. But I never wanted to be alone. There must be wolves somewhere. If only I knew which way to turn.

I stop on a ridgetop at midday. I find a sheltered spot between boulders where the tall grasses cover me. A pair of vultures soars back and forth on the rising air. The drowsy hum of bees lulls me to sleep. In my dream, I hear the far-off drumming of hooves. In my dream, elk are running toward me, more elk than I could ever eat, and wolves following after them. They come closer and closer, and when they are almost close enough to touch, I startle awake—alone on a bare windy mountaintop.

They were so close! I bark a hopeful call even

though I know it was only a dream. Echoes come back to tease me. My head slumps to the ground. How can there be so much land and no wolves? I heave a sigh and then . . . I feel the ground tremble.

I listen-smell all around me, but there is no hint of elk. I keep my neck and chin pressed flat to the rock. The ground trembles like it does when elk are on the move. I am not dreaming. The shiver on the skin of the earth grows. There is no elk smell. After a while, I can hear the hoofbeats coming up the mountain. They sound wrong. Something is off about the rhythm. I get to my feet but keep low and ready to run, in case there is trouble. I listen for the high-pitched calls elk make when they travel, but all I can hear is low, snorting grunts. Very strange. Whatever they are, there are many of them. I see their cloud of dust first and then they come over the rise—horses!

Horses are the pack mates of men; they always came into our mountains together. They took food from each other. I look-smell for men. The usual trap that sticks a man to a horse's back is gone. The lead horse is rounder than the rest, and the one at the back is the tallest. When they come to the open meadow below me, they slow to a walk and then stop to graze. The two smallest nip at each other's necks and have a race around the others.

The tall one walks around the edge of the meadow, smelling the wind for trouble. He keeps an eye on the wrestling match, and when the yearlings get too close to the sheer cliff at one end of the meadow, he nudges them away from danger and settles their fight with one well-placed nip. He's the father of the pack, plain to see. The horses are all coyote colored, with black manes, tails, and legs, and one long stripe down the back. The leader of the group, the fattest of them, circles the meadow until she finds a patch of snow in the shadow of an overhanging rock. She kicks a few chunks free and nibbles a drink of snow. Then she goes back to pacing in slower and slower circles.

There is something odd about the lead horse's smell. It's almost like the red that runs from an elk when you kill it. But not quite. It's a little bit like the dark goo that runs out of the guts when you bite into them. But that is not right either. I am certain I have never smelled this before. The father can smell it too. He curls his upper lip back and breathes it in. He moves close to the lead horse and talks to her gently. He nose-touches her and lets her rest against his shoulder. I cannot look away from their tenderness. It reminds me of Warm and our days together in the den. I hold completely still in the tall grass and watch.

The smell that I cannot figure out grows stronger. It is a wild smell, a sharp smell, and something about it makes me hungry. The round horse walks more and more slowly. She lies down in the grass and then gets up. Water and a little bit of red runs down her back legs. Could she be sick? She lies down one more time, and the father stands guard over her. The other horses come around one by one and touch noses with her. Something is going on here. The lying-down horse starts to shudder. The smell grows more pungent every moment, and I see more water spilling out. Something is definitely going on here, and it might be something delicious. I sit on my wag and wait.

The father gives encouraging snorts and grunts. After a while, a great bulge comes out of the back of the horse—a sticky black bulge. It is the most disgusting, fascinating thing I have ever seen. I cannot look away.

The lying-down horse breathes in great shuddering breaths. The black bulge grows longer and stickier. This is not like any sickness I have ever seen. And still the father stands watch, faithful and strong. Shadows grow longer and the air cools. A sprinkle of rain falls. I lick the drops from the long grass, but still I cannot stop watching. The horse struggles to stand. She gets halfway up only to flop back down as her bulge grows longer and longer.

And then the slimy black thing splits open. Two feet! Feet with hooves and knees that bend. I cannot believe it! There is a tiny horse inside the bulge. And the mother is having this little horse right in the middle of her family—no den, no burrow. Nothing.

All her family is right there, watching and talking to her, touching her nose to nose. The grunts and cries go on, and then a head comes out all wrapped in the same sack that covers the legs. The father nips at the sack, and the head breaks free. The mother tries to half stand, and the rest of it comes out in a whoosh of waters and a burst of delicious smell.

HUNT

My stomach gurgles in anticipation. Pups are tasty. Everybody knows it. When I was learning to hunt, Growl showed me how to take down a deer pup, just in case I was ever alone and hunting with a limp like him. It was sweet and tender, the bones so easy to crack, and the tasty middles of the bone fresher than any I had ever eaten before.

The mother horse licks her pup, eating up the sack of skin that he was born in as she goes. The father rears up and gives a call that is full of the victory of new life. Something about his voice makes me shiver with dread. He gallops a wide circle around the meadow, shaking his mane back and forth over his broad shoulders. He makes steaming, smelly piles to mark his home ground. I take a good look at those hooves and remember the elk that almost killed me. The sound of my own bones cracking rings clear in my memory. My shoulder aches to think of it, and I lick the white mark on my skin for comfort. This father of horses is not as tall as an elk, but he is just as broad and strong. His golden-brown coat shines in the slant of afternoon sunlight. One kick from him, and I might never walk again. I want no quarrel with him.

The rest of the horses come up to the newborn. They nose-touch and speak softly. They stroke the mother's sweaty neck and sides. They urge her to stand. They walk around and around her, never stepping on the little one as it lies drying on the ground. They are careful and kind—a pack, just like mine. The father looks at his family and snorts with pride.

I want this. Not just any pack that will take

me in. I want to lead a pack. I always wanted to be the boss of Sharp, just to prove that being the fastest matters more than being the biggest. I always wanted to look after Warm and hunt for him and keep him safe. But this is more. So much more. I want home ground. I want to wet-mark a place of my own, a good place, full of trees and elk. I want snow

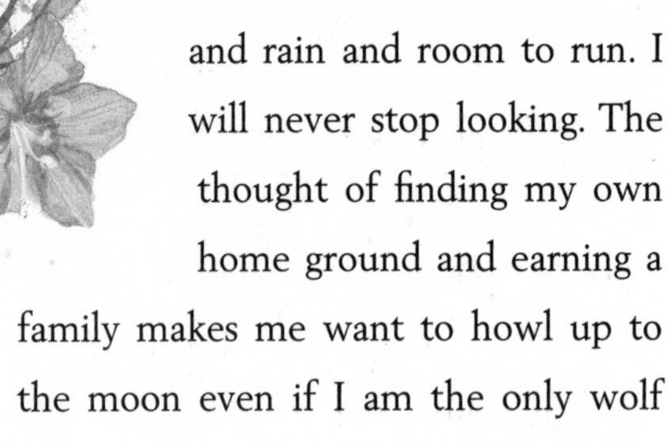

and rain and room to run. I will never stop looking. The thought of finding my own home ground and earning a family makes me want to howl up to the moon even if I am the only wolf howling.

This is no time for a howl. I should move on. I should leave the horses in peace. The sun has hit the horizon, and I use the last of the light to choose a path off the mountain, a path that will not cross the meadow, the horses' home ground. I am about to go when I hear a rock behind me roll downhill. Instantly, I am on my feet and wary. I did not smell anyone coming. Did not hear anyone. That can only mean one thing—a hunter is nearby. I scan the boulder field behind me and find it. A cougar. The pup-stealer!

Mother's first warning was about cougars. She took us to a line of cougar tracks in the forest. We memorized the shape of the print and the smell. Mother described the color of the fur and the markings on the face.

"He is the silent hunter," she said. "He climbs trees. He attacks from behind, and always—always—he steals the young. Beware!"

I look over my shoulder at the horses in the meadow. They are settling in for the night, wrapped in the warmth of the new pup and each other. Even the father is weary and puts his head down to rest. They have no ravens to send up the alarm.

I check my escape route. I am no little pup to be stolen in the night. The new horse is what a cougar would want. I should walk away. But the horses are not sneaking, solitary creatures. They are not mindless grass-eaters like sheep. They are a pack. I could warn them. I should.

A cougar is bigger than me. He can jump rivers I have to swim, and leap into trees like a bird. With a pack at my side I would not fear him for a moment, but I am on my own and cougars are treacherous. It is coming into range. In a moment, smell will give me away. I make my choice.

I give one sharp bark. It is all the warning I

can spare. I bolt from the ridgetop. I am fast, but a cougar is faster in the short run. I pour on the speed, taking the steepest route I can find.

The father is up in an instant. He gives an answering cry. He drums the ground with his hooves. The whole pack responds. I hear them galloping circles around the little one. They call their threats to the cougar, their voices joining together, almost a howl. I do not hear the death cry of a stolen pup. The cougar has left the horses alone.

It must be hunting me now. I zig and zag, looking over my shoulder. A cougar can run as silent as a shadow. I will never hear it coming. I am ready to fight if it comes to teeth and claws. I leap over boulders. The horses are far behind me. I cannot even smell them. I put all my hope in speed. My paws pound down the mountain, straight down. I keep to open ground, where I will not be taken by a leap from an overhanging ledge. I do not smell the cougar following me, but I will not slacken my pace.

I run full out past the tree line. Through the

clumps of junipers and the sagebrush. Back on the flat ground, I keep running. The last light of day glows gold against the white trunks of aspens. I swerve to one side and look back, still running. Nothing is moving in the twilight. The air all around me is clean of cougar smell. If my raven were with me, she would raise the alarm. Now I have no one but myself. I put my faith in endurance. Cougars are fast, but no one has stamina like a wolf. I make space between me and trouble. It is fully dark when I slow to a trot and then a walk.

Luck was with me this time, but I will not try that trick again. Not for a pack that is not my own. I keep walking through the night, alone again, but grateful to be alive.

TRACK

The wolf star rises behind me. I turn and look back. I tell myself Mother's story.

"The pack belongs to the mountains and the mountains belong to the pack, and the wolf star watches us all."

I keep looking until the stars fade and the horizon shimmers with gold. I could go home. I could retrace my steps. I could brave the black river and cross it one more time. I could follow my own scent marks and go back to the mountains I love and the elk I need.

The breeze picks up. In the tall grass around me,

little yellow birds cling to the stalks as they bend and sway. They chirp and whistle and trill together, like a pack howling. I can still hear my own pack howling in my dreams. I remember how it felt to lift up my head and sing. Ripples of sound washed over me like water. I remember feeling, when the howl was done, that there was nothing we couldn't do together.

But my pack is gone. If I went back to the mountains, I would have to fight my way into the pale wolves' pack. I am leaner than before. Now that my shoulder has healed, I am as fast as ever. But I was not the heaviest one in the pack when I left. I turn away from the sunrise. Returning is no answer for a wolf like me.

I hear the trickle of a spring and follow the sound to where it bubbles up from stones. I lap up cold water and then follow the creek until it becomes a bigger stream. Something good to eat will come to drink. I only have to wait. The bank is crisscrossed with the footprints of mice. I drink again and then look for cover to rest under. I find a shrub and a patch of shade. The sound of the water is soothing. I will doze through the heat of the day and then eat when the deer come at sundown. I stretch my weary legs and yawn. In that intake of breath, I catch the faintest taste of . . . can it be?

I raise my nose to the air, but this scent is coming from the ground. A trail. A wolf trail! I know it! I leap-spin like a pup and then follow it, nose to the dirt and all my fatigue forgotten. It leads me downstream. In the mud I find it, a perfect print: four claw points, four toes, and a pad as big as mine. I breathe in the smell of the footfall. There is something familiar. It is so long since I have been with another wolf. I breathe in deeply and close my eyes to remember. It is a female. Not my sisters, not my mother, but I have smelled this wolf before. Could it be the stranger wolf from the far side of the black river? Did she find a way across it? Has she been looking for me all this time?

My first impulse is to track her. These marks

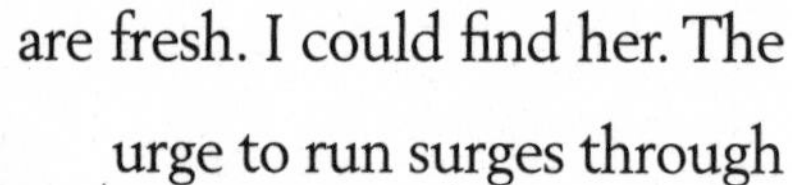

are fresh. I could find her. The urge to run surges through me. But I stop. I take another hard look at the stranger wolf's print and my paw beside it. She is not small. She might even be bigger than me. Pounce was. I look-smell for other wolves in her pack. I crisscross the whole area to be sure. There is only this one wolf's print. Only one scat. Only one smell. If this wolf has survived alone out here, then she is tougher than all my sisters put together. I will have to win her respect.

"A lead wolf feeds his pack," Mother always said. "Nothing else matters."

All I have to do is set a feast for her. I will make a kill—such a kill. I will open the hide and spread choice bits around the body. Vultures will come. And then hawks and ravens. They will announce my great deed, and she will come running. She will duck her head to me and beg for a share. Yes! I can see it. I can taste it already.

But this will take patience. I have learned this on my journey: tired is stupid. I must rest, or I'll make mistakes I regret. A meal will come to me if I wait by the water.

I turn back to my cover and lie down in the shade. I get up again and take a quick dust bath. I duck my face under the water and let the stream carry away the grit of my travels. I should look like a lead wolf when I meet her.

Tiny birds, yellow, tan, and gray, flit up and down the river, catching flies as I rest. A speckled fish leaps clear of the water. My ears perk up at midday when I hear the footsteps of deer cautiously working their way to water. The urge to hunt washes over me, making my heart run fast. I am stronger now than I have ever been.

A new kind of deer comes to the stream to drink. There are many. They are small and tan with white bellies and bottoms and broad, striped faces. Their

horns are short and black. Maybe I have not found other wolves before because I've been taking little animals out of need, and not deer and elk like a wolf should.

I will kill this black-horned deer. Father would want me to. I can never get him back, but I can make him live in my hunting. I will howl his song over the meat. The stranger wolf will come to me. If I feed her, she will follow me like Mother and Song and Growl followed him. If I feed her again, she will follow me again, and if I feed her all

through the winter, she will never leave me.

I pick out the finest buck in the group. His black horns have two prongs. As he leans down to drink I spring forward, closing the ground between us. The others scatter in all directions, but I have marked my meat. He runs like a falcon dives, straight and fast, with no thought but speed. I stretch out the length of my strides, covering the ground between us. I can smell his fear. I will bring him down. It is the only trick I need. I watch for fatigue to make the strange deer stumble, but he runs on as water runs, smoothly, easily, dodging around rocks with no effort.

The day heats up, but I have taken plenty of water. I can run until sundown. I leap the shrubs he dodges around. The stream is far behind me now. We both run with our mouths open. The dry air wearies me. But there will be plenty to drink when the buck falls.

He keeps running. I match him stride for stride. He kicks up puffs of gritty dust. I keep pace but cannot pull ahead. I look for a trap to drive the buck into—a creek, a cleft in a rock, a thick cluster of shrubs. The water is far behind us now, and there is nothing on the horizon but pale tufts of grass and sagebrush.

I am tired, but I will run forever if that's what it takes. Even so, the black-horned buck pulls ahead. My feet pound the ground in time to my heart: front, front, back, back. And still the strange deer runs on, as swift as I am strong. There is no catching him. My heart aches and I am gasping. I slow to a trot and then to a walk, huffing dust out of my nose. My feast is gone. My hope of finding the stranger wolf, gone with it. Why would she stay with a wolf that can't take down the smallest deer there is?

I find a long-eared rabbit hiding in a dip in the ground underneath a sagebrush. In one pounce I have him, and in three bites he's gone. Coyote food. I hang my head and kick up dust as I walk. For the first time I am glad Father is not here to see me. Glad he doesn't know what kind of wolf I have become. A wolf who deserves to be alone.

I trot onward, looking for a clump of junipers, some shade to rest in. Nothing. Yellow dirt. Red dirt. Black dirt. This is no land for a wolf. Maybe a fox, willing to live on mice and rabbits alone, could make a life on this bare ground. I drop to a walk but keep going. The sun makes its own walk across the sky, and my shadow is all the company I find.

I rest in the hottest part of the day and then

keep walking as the sun sinks. I cannot bear to search the sky for the wolf star. A half-moon stands above me, and I am half a wolf in its light—no elk, no mountains, no pack. I throw back my head to howl, but my throat is empty.

RUN

I walk on through the night and into the morning. I zigzag across the desert looking for some trace of the stranger wolf. There is no sign of her. I do not know where to go. I only know that the ground under my feet could never be home ground to me. I could survive on it, but I could never love it like I love the mist-covered mountains of home. I lift my head to pick up the scent of the stranger wolf.

She could be anywhere from horizon to horizon. I walk-trot-run-rest all day, but there is no trace—no track of her paw, no scent in the air, not even a gathering of hawks and crows to mark where she has hunted. I miss my raven as I have not missed her since I left the lakeshore. I press on through the night, looking by ear and nose. For days, I keep searching. She is here somewhere. I call for her, and only silence comes back. I cannot find even the company of an echo.

When the sun rises again, I see iron-gray mountains ahead. Mountains! They will have trees and meadows and elk. Mountains will have cool air and elk. Soft needles to rest on and elk. Cold water to drink, and endless packs of deer and elk. If there are any wolves in this wide, empty land, they will be in the mountains. If the stranger wolf sees the mountains, she will want them as much as I do. I journey on, my hope rekindled.

All day the mountains grow taller, rounder, and darker. The wind picks up. As I go on, the grasses become taller and thicker and the ground softer. I come to a pool to drink, but the water smells sour and warm steam rises from it. I peer into the depths of the pool, but nothing alive is in there. I'll drink somewhere else.

By evening I can see they are not mountains, but clouds. Only clouds. They are tall and dark and full of rain. I do not give up. Rain clouds gather in front of mountains as ravens gather over a kill. And the smell of rain, even rain that has not fallen, gives me courage. I lope toward the clouds and they come toward me. I can taste the water in the air and feel it on my skin, but the rain does not fall. The wind blows harder, throwing bits of grass in the air, and thunder rolls, but still no rain. I travel through the night with the sound of thunder on all sides. Flashes of lightning dazzle my eyes.

Fire weather, Growl would call it. On a summer day when a plume of smoke rose up from the forest after lightning, he would gather us pups together and tell us about the fire that made him lame, about the patch on his rear quarter where fur would not grow again, about the run of his life.

"Fire doesn't care how brave you are," Growl would say.

"Fire doesn't care how strong you are," he would say again, because Sharp was never listening. He would go on and on.

"Fire runs up a slope."

"Fire waits a moment at the top of a ridge."

And always, always, "You must seek water."

I sample the air. In front of me, the air is clean, but a steady headwind hides all smells behind me. And there is no lake to shelter in if fire comes. I can only hope for rain. I dream of rain when I stop to rest. I can smell it in my memory, but rain does not fall.

In the morning the clouds are taller and blacker than before, but they have passed behind me. I press on, more thirsty than hungry. Along the horizon is a rising ridge, darker than the rest. Mountains? I have been fooled before, but I journey on with hope.

By midday the wind swings around and brings

the sound of thunder and great crackling claps of lightning. My fur stands on end. The pulse of sound pushes me onward. There is still no rain. I listen and smell for it. No rain, but another sound—a steady roar and pop. I turn and see smoke.

Smoke!

A wash of dread flashes through me from nose to tail. It freezes my paws to the ground while I search for an escape route. Smoke can fool you. It steals away your smell, slows your run, and chokes your breath. It hides the safe path from you and makes you fall. The fire behind the smoke is even worse. It can roar like a bear and run just as fast, but if you turn to fight it, there is nothing to sink your teeth into. The bitter taste of fear is deep in my throat. There are things a wolf can fight and things he can't.

I must run, but where? If my raven were here, she'd show me a path. All I can see is parched grass and tumbleweeds and junipers in every direction, and the hint of hills on the sunset horizon. Water

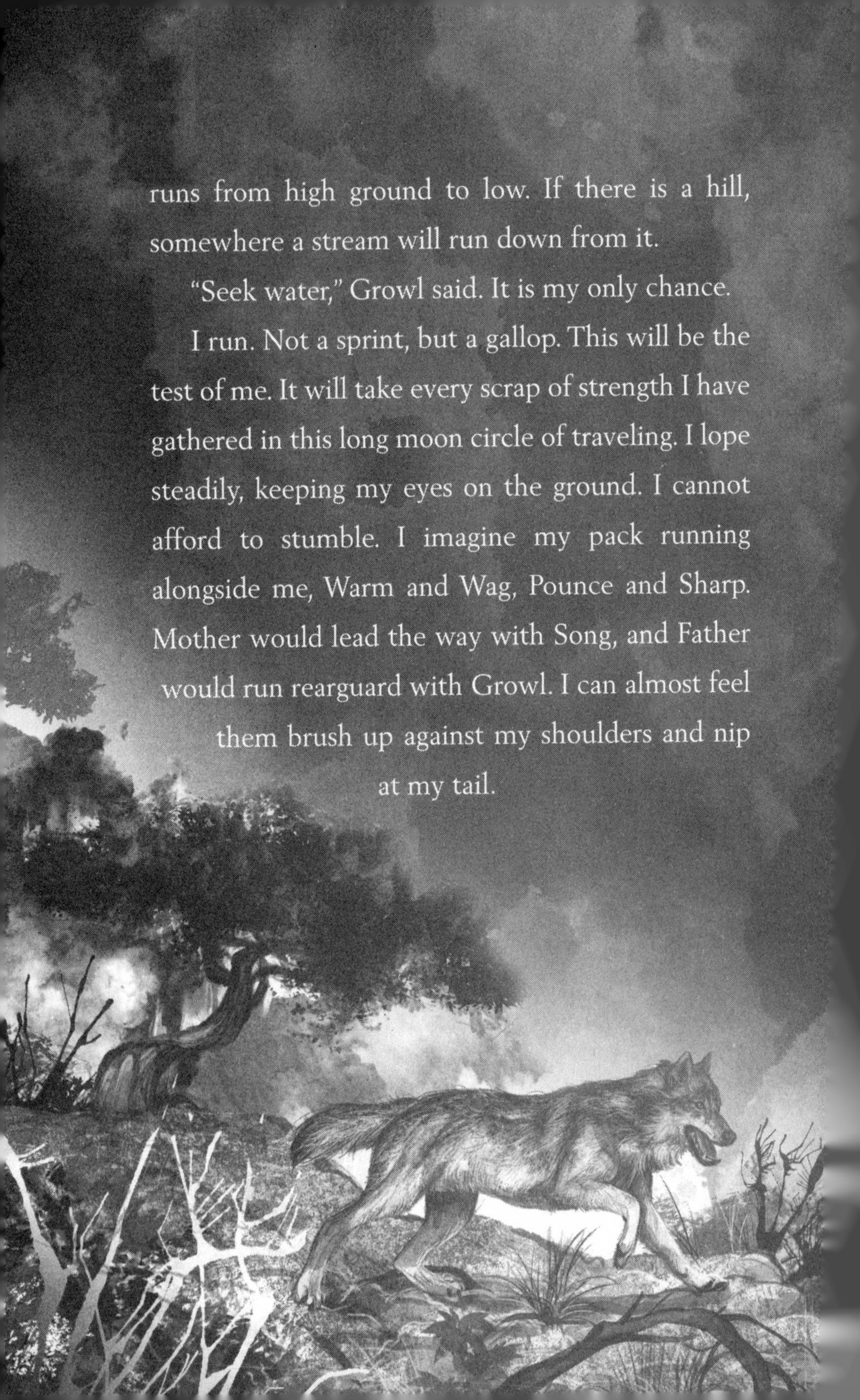

runs from high ground to low. If there is a hill, somewhere a stream will run down from it.

"Seek water," Growl said. It is my only chance.

I run. Not a sprint, but a gallop. This will be the test of me. It will take every scrap of strength I have gathered in this long moon circle of traveling. I lope steadily, keeping my eyes on the ground. I cannot afford to stumble. I imagine my pack running alongside me, Warm and Wag, Pounce and Sharp. Mother would lead the way with Song, and Father would run rearguard with Growl. I can almost feel them brush up against my shoulders and nip at my tail.

Never give up, they say to me.

You are the fastest of us all.

I will follow you anywhere.

Carry on. Carry on. Carry on.

The roar of the fire grows. A bitter smell billows around me. The wind that pushes the fire pushes the smoke ahead of it. The hills grow larger on the horizon. Two of the shimmering green birds zip past me. They hover for a moment and rest on my shoulders. They weigh nothing at all, but I can feel the flutter of their tiny hearts. It gives me courage. A few moments' rest, and they are on their way, two green streaks of lightning. I mark their path and follow it. The smoke turns the sun amber and then red and then earth brown. The bitter smell of it clings to my fur and scalds my throat. Birds crowd the sky ahead of the fire, crows and songbirds, eagles and cranes. They fly low, and I follow them.

My nose and ears tell me the fire is closer. I blink stinging grit out of my eyes and keep running. The black-horned deer appear out of the smoke beside me, their long tan-and-white necks stretched forward as they run. Tiny gray horses, with their big ears twitching in panic, appear like ghosts on my other side. They run in a pack. Yesterday they would be food, but today I wish them life. I feel the ground rise, and through the haze of smoke I see shrubs and a few thin-trunked alders and aspens. They are the first taste of bigger things to come. I press on, breathing hard. Jackrabbits and coyotes run side by side like pack mates.

The smoke confuses my smell. The roar of fire drowns out everything I might hear. The fire leaps ahead of me on one side. It crackles though the grass. It hunts the juniper trees, climbing up them with a great whoosh and a bang as the trunk pops open and a shower of sparks rains down. The air shimmers with heat, and I swerve away from the flames. As I climb into the hills, the pale trunks of alder and birch appear in the smoky twilight.

They are streamside trees. I can only trust that they are marking the path to water.

Rising ground slows me down, but fire does not mind a slope. It picks up the pace. I bite back panic and run flat out, ears back and heart pounding. There must be water somewhere! The roar of the fire is all around me. I hear the snap and boom of burning trunks, the crackle and hiss of burning needles. Fire leaps from one tree to the next, raining down sparks and flaming branches. I dodge away. Another burning branch flies through the air and lands on my path. I dodge again. Flames light up the smoke-darkened sky and cast flickering shadows.

My shoulder begins to ache as the land rises more steeply. There is a ridgeline ahead. I make for it, hoping Growl was right. Sparks eat into my fur like biting flies. A rabbit running beside me stumbles, rolls ears-over-tail to a stop. I do not stop, but I hear him scream. Runners around me stumble. I fight to keep my feet.

The wind lifts burning weeds and grass and

branches swirling into the air. They form a great spinning plume of fire taller than trees, taller than clouds. It sweeps across my path. I duck away and it swirls toward me again, cutting off my escape. It lights the grass as it goes, putting me in the center of a circle of fire. I skid to a stop. Heat presses me on all sides. My nose and lips blister and crack. Everywhere I turn, there is no escape. My throat is too dry for a howl, too dry for even a whimper.

Carry on.

My father's voice is in the beating of my heart. I am desperate to go, but which way? I turn and turn again. I cannot see beyond the flames.

Carry on.

I will not bow down to this fire. I cannot. Even as the unburned circle of grass where I stand grows smaller. I squeeze my eyes shut against the wind. The ground under my feet slopes down. Water will flow down. I turn to the downhill side of the ring. Eyes still closed, I gather myself for a great spring. I burst through the swirling circle of fire. I hit the ground on a downhill slope. I roll over and over in the dirt until the smell of burning fur is gone. I spring to my feet and run. The fire is on my heels, scorching my paws. Fire is above my head, singeing my fur. Burning branches topple and light up more trees. The ground gets steeper, and I pour on the speed.

Carry on. Carry on.

I promise it to my father, my pack, myself.

Above the tornado of fire I cannot hear or see or smell water, but it must be there at the bottom of the ravine. I press forward, stumble, roll to my feet, and run again. And there it is. Not just a stream, but a river. A river! I fall in.

Ah! Sweet relief! I duck all the way under, killing every spark in my fur. Cooling, soothing, saving water. At last. I swim downstream, around a bend to a wider spot in the river with a broad sandy bank on one side and bare rocks on the other.

We stand in the water together—coyotes, deer, rabbits. Though I am hungry, I cannot stir the desire to hunt. Fire rages up to the water's edge. Burning trees pop, crack, and topple into the river with great hisses of steam. The heat is blistering. I duck in up to my shoulders. The river runs fast and cold and true. I have never been so grateful for water.

In the fire's yellow-orange light, I look among all the animals for the amber eyes and black ears of the stranger wolf. The smoke is so thick I cannot

even smell the buck standing right beside me. I search in the strange midday twilight of soot and ash. Black-horned deer stand dazed, their sides heaving from the run. Songbirds rest on their shoulders, completely spent. Beside them stand a bear and her pup. Two small gray horses with long ears nuzzle each other for comfort. Many have survived, but the stranger wolf is not here.

All this time, all this long time, she was traveling, alone, just like me, and I never found her.

At the water's edge, the fire burns out. One moment the flames are shoulder-high and crackling, and then they are snuffed out. Trees and shrubs still glow with fire, but the grass is gone. Devoured. Nothing of it remains but smoke and a shimmer of heat.

In time the smoke thins, revealing a moon nearly full. In its light, the rabbits and voles and squirrels scatter. Coyotes and foxes wade out of the river after them, still in a daze, the drive to hunt not yet taking hold. Ashes rain down, leaving a bitter tang when I drink. The deer step slowly and gracefully to the far shore. They shake off fear and melt into the silver shadows of trees. I drink deeply in spite of the bitter taste. I walk up the green bank alone on the far side of the river. I drop to the ground, lick my scorched paws, and fall asleep.

HOWL

The smell of smoke wakes me with a start. I spring to my feet, wincing as my scorched paws hit the ground. I look-spin. The smell of smoke is everywhere, but there are no flames in sight. I shake the ash out of my fur. Look to the river for any sign that the fire has crossed. There is no roar and pop of flames, only the steady rush of the river. The sun rises rusty orange through the haze. I blink away the sting of smoke and bark black soot out of my mouth. I look-spin again, slowly this time. The deer and rabbits and birds—all the animals from the river yesterday—are gone. I drop my chin to the ground, and a puff of ash rises out of the grass and pine needles. They will not eat this grass, not until the rain has washed it clean. I stretch, bone-weary, turn twice, and flop back down on the ash-crunchy grass.

I sleep and wake and sleep again, long into the day. I yawn and stretch as the sun falls down behind the mountains. By moonrise the wind shifts, carrying the smoke back over the burned ground. Floating ash and soot move on, and the river water tastes sweet again. I drink my fill and then gaze at the scorched earth on the far side. It is black as far as I can see. If the stranger wolf is out there, she is once again on the opposite shore. There is no tracking over burned ground. I will never find her.

The moon is bright enough to cast shadows. It was last full like this when the pale wolves came over the mountains to kill my family. I have journeyed so far since then. I am not that wolf anymore.

I follow the river with a heavy heart, but with each step these mountains feel more like home. My old friends, the pines and firs, greet me. And huckleberries! They are not quite ripe, but I can smell the bears that have come by to check on them. The air is cooler as I climb. I can smell the homes of rabbits and ground squirrels. Deer trails meander from one meadow to the next. I rub up against the familiar bark of a hemlock tree as if greeting a pack mate. I top the ridgeline, and cooler, moister air meets me, swirling from one rocky peak to the next. Mountain upon mountain stands before me, and my heart soars at the sight of them.

There are new trees here, and smells I have never met before. Something little and dark brown, like a weasel but with a duck's webbed feet, hunts fish in the creek bed below me. A chubby, wet wormy thing with legs darts in and out of its hole to eat spiders. I could watch that trick all night. I walk on, breathing in the new and the unfamiliar smells until I stumble upon a gigantic tree. It smells like no other. It is thick trunked and the color of fox fur.

The needles fan out like a bird's wing. I look up and up and up. Eagles could not find the top of this tree. A chill runs through me at the sight of it. I lower my tail and nose-touch it with respect—the father of trees. I curl up to rest in the soft, springy tree droppings. The familiar deep hoots of the big owl and the short, high screeches of the little owl keep me company through the night.

Thinking of my family, I search the homeward horizon for the wolf star. It will rise just ahead of the sun. I miss my family more than I have missed them my whole journey long. They should be here with me. I have been running all this time, wildly hoping that someone survived. Hoping they would find my tracks and follow them. And now at last I've found a place where we could live as wolves should. And I am all alone. The stars make their slow walk up the sky, and just as the wolf star steps above the horizon, I hear a howl.

A howl!

I jump to my feet and drink in the sound. It is magnificent—none of the yipping and yapping coyotes make. Not the grunts of a bear, not the yowls of a cougar. Nothing but long, clear *oo*OOO*ooo* that echoes from the hills. It makes my fur stand on end. I turn to face the voice. I lift my head to smell for its maker. The wind is blowing the wrong way for smelling, but the voice . . . it cannot be far.

I am hungry for companionship like I have never been hungry for meat. A moon cycle ago, I would have run to greet it without a second thought. But I have journeyed too far to make that mistake now. It could be a friend out there in the darkness, lonely and searching just like me. Or it could be a lookout, the messenger of a pack hidden somewhere nearby, a pack ready to kill me if I step onto their home ground.

I listen and wait. At sunup, the wolf howls again. No other voices join in. I head in the direction of the new wolf, but I look-smell for the scent marks of a pack's territory. I search out high ground. I think about escape routes.

There is no border to find. No mark of rival wolves. I make my choice and run toward the new wolf. As I run, I hear the rat-a-tat call of woodpeckers and the squawk of the black-headed blue jay. Chubby, short-eared brush rabbits, so different from the long, lanky rabbits of the desert, dart for cover as I run by. All of it reminds me of home. Not everything is the same. There are trees I can't name. Birds I have never seen before. But it is like home. It could be home.

As I draw close to where I heard the howling, I look-smell for tracks. I zigzag through the trees and find a smell I have not smelled since I left home.

Elk.

Not one. Many.

Suddenly I am hungry, but not because I haven't eaten today. I am hungry because elk is food. Real

food. Wolf food. And in that instant, I make up my mind. This will be my home ground, my mountains. Whether this new wolf will have me or not. Everything I need is here. I stand up against a pine tree and mark with my claws as high as I can reach. I wet-mark it.

Not the faint gentle smell-marks my feet make. Not the marks that say, Here I am. Follow if you like.

This mark says, MINE. Mine for living. Mine for hunting. Mine until you kill me to take it away.

PACK

I am ready now. I howl to the new wolf. I put all my strength and all my hopes into the howl. The echo of it rings from the mountaintops. And into the silence that follows comes a lower, sweeter howl. I drink in the sound, and in my joy I almost answer back in the tail-wagging yips of a pup. I stop myself midwag and give a dignified howl—a howl that would do my pack proud. The new wolf howls right back. I lift my head and taste the wind. Yes! She is on the ridge across from me. A good night's run. I would not care if it were ten nights' run, I will not stop until I find her. I take the ground between us like a bird takes the sky.

I remember when Father came home from the hunt, we all crowded up to him, bowing our heads and lowering our tails. He went among us, tapping each of us on the head, showing us that we belonged to the pack, promising to always feed us. I want to be a wolf like my father for this new wolf. I have not even met her, and already I want to take care of her. Hunt for her. Protect her.

I work my way down the ridge and into the valley between us. There are elk to hunt, there is home ground to mark, a den to dig, and a night sky waiting to be filled with howling. I work my way up the opposite side. She calls out to me again, and again from the same place. She is guiding me to her. Hope rises in me, and I sprint the last upward stretch. The fox-colored trees with the bird-wing needles are thick on the ground here, and ferns and huckleberries. One last call, so close, and there she is—a raven-black wolf pacing in a meadow before me. A black wolf with amber eyes. I breathe in her scent, remembering. It is the stranger wolf from the far side of the black river. I would know her anywhere. I hold still, practically holding my breath, just to look at her.

I woof to her.

She is so beautiful I can't look away.

I woof softly to her again. "I have traveled a long way to find you."

I stand my tallest. I hold up my ears and tail and walk toward her.

She holds my gaze and growl-woofs in return.

She holds her ears and tail up tall. She is big. The closer I come, the more I see that she is just as tall as me, and as broad in the shoulder. The young wolf that ran away from his home ground would have been afraid. But I have left that wolf far behind. I am more than Swift now. Speed is not the only thing I have to offer. I have covered more ground than my mother or father ever did. I have seen new animals, new trees, birds they never met and lands they never traveled.

"Call me Wander," I say.

"Night," she answers. "I am Night."

She is glossy black from nose to tail. Her beauty takes my breath away. But she does not duck her head or lower her tail, not even for the briefest flick.

This is not how I thought this would go.

I stop. My father was the settled leader of our pack. He never showed me how to meet a grown wolf for the first time. I take a step. Stop again.

She keeps looking at me with those unblinking amber eyes, and I cannot break away from her gaze. I take another step.

She does not lower her tail to me.

I try all the tricks that worked on my sisters. I bark a command. I pound the ground with my front paws. Warm bowed to me always, and Wag sometimes, and in the end, when we were full grown, I could even get Pounce to lower her tail—but this wolf, this Night, will not budge. I do not know what to do next.

Night takes a step toward me. And another.

Her tail is as tall as ever. It waves from side to side. I cannot stop looking at it, though a smart wolf would be watching her teeth. It could be a trick. I should be careful, but the smell of her is good—so good. I give my deepest growl and drum the ground again.

She lowers her head and chest, but this is no crouch of a following wolf. She is getting ready to spring. I crouch as well, and when we spring together

it is like the elk that crash head-to-head in battle. I run the length of the meadow with Night behind me so close I can feel her breath. I spin-snarl at the edge of the meadow and chase her back. She is fast and strong. We sprint round and round the meadow, first her leading and then me. She is wild and fierce, a born hunter.

If she will have me, I will never be hungry again.

Overhead I hear the call of a raven. I stop to listen, and so does Night. A raven comes and lands on the bowed head of a hemlock tree, raining down needles on us both. I know it is not my raven, but it comforts me to find her kin here after all my travels. I promise myself that I will listen to ravens as my father did and his father before him. I see that Night is listening too. I cannot take my eyes off her. I take a step toward her in silence, ears up and tail level. She steps toward me. I take a step, and she takes another.

Our noses touch.

A shiver passes through me from ears to tail. Night takes one step closer and rests her head on my shoulder. I rub my head against her neck and lick her ears.

"Will you hunt?" she says.

"Yes."

"Elk?" she says.

"Yes."

"Always?"

"Yes!"

I run with her, pain forgotten and long journey forgotten and all my loneliness forgotten. We pause on the ridgeline to listen-smell. Then run silently, looking for the open clearings where elk like to feed. We pick up a scent in the same moment, and Night knows what to do without being told. She leads the stalking of the elk, picks the sheltered approach. We pause to watch, noticing a yearling buck that has wandered to the edge of the group. I lead the chase, cutting him off from the rest of his pack, turning him again and again to keep him on open ground. We make the killing blow together. The elk falls. I make a final bite to the throat to still its kicking legs.

We stand over our meal, red running from our mouths, and she knows. She waits. Just for a moment. To be grateful for the life we have taken. In that moment I'm more grateful for the life I've found than the one I've taken. She still will not lower her tail to me, and I suspect she never will. But she has not made me lower my tail to her either. An equal bond. Like Mother and Father.

When we have eaten our fill of the elk and left a share for coyotes and ravens, I am fuller than food alone could ever make me. We walk back to our home meadow and mark each tree, one on top of the other. Not mine, not only mine. Ours.

All through the heat of summer and into the snowy bliss of winter, we hunt side by side. There are elk aplenty and streams full of clear water to drink. Some days we run in the snow for the pure joy of running. We fill the nights with howling, and we faithfully mark the borders of our home ground. But there is no threatening howl from an enemy pack. There is only one black river, and very seldom does the stench of men come into our forest. Men are easy to avoid as we roam the ridges and valleys and hidden lakes of our mountains. This is how a wolf should live.

Even so, some days I search out the sunrise side of our mountains and look back. I remember Warm. I send my howl to him on the wind, not because I think he can hear me. I call to him because in my heart I want to believe that he is on a mountainside somewhere, with good wolves all around him and

plenty of elk to eat. I want to believe that even in his happiness, he will always look for me. The smell-memory of my brother has followed me all this way, across rivers and deserts and mountains and burned ground. I breathe in the memory, knowing that we will always, and never, be together.

Winter holds the mountains in its frozen grip, but as the days grow long, it melts into spring. Night becomes quiet and more mysterious than before. She digs a den deep in the most hidden valley of our home ground. We line it with grass together, and then she hides herself away from me. For days and days. I hunt alone and bring her the best of everything. I do not howl, cannot howl, while she is hidden from me, but I watch for the wolf star on the morning horizon. I wait and hope. The moon swells from a sliver to a circle, and just when I think my Night will never come back to me, I hear voices deep inside the den. My Night and three voices more.

Our pups begin in darkness, but my nose tells

me they are mine. Ours. A pack of our own. I nose-touch my thanks to Night. I lick all three pups from ears to tail, memorizing every squirming bit of them. Every step of my journey was for this, beautiful this. I lift up my head and sing their names to the wolf star that watches us all.

THE REAL WOLF BEHIND THE STORY

This story is inspired by the life and travels of a real Oregon wolf called OR-7. He was born into the Imnaha pack in the Wallowa Mountains in northeastern Oregon. Biologists fitted OR-7 with a radio collar—this allowed them to track his movement, to help protect livestock, and to learn more about how wolves behave.

OR-7 was photographed by a trail camera in May 2014

Oregon is home to many black wolves,
and OR- 7's mate has a black coat like this one

In September 2011, when OR-7 was about two years old, he left his home and traveled more than a thousand miles, through eastern and southern Oregon and into northern California. Although he passed through cattle- and sheep-ranching territory along the way, he didn't kill any livestock. OR-7 ended his journey in the Siskiyou

National Forest region of the Cascade Range, a habitat similar to the one he grew up in, a region rich in deer and elk. There he found a mate where no other wolf had been seen for nearly seventy years. In 2014, the pair had

Wolf pups emerging from their den

at least three pups who survived their first winter, and in the summer of 2015, when the pair had a second litter of pups, they were named the Rogue Pack, because they live in the Rogue River watershed. OR-7 was given the name Journey in a naming contest involving schoolchildren around the world. As of this writing, Journey is about ten years old—a brilliant accomplishment for a wild wolf. Most don't live half as long. He and his mate had a fifth litter of pups in the spring of 2018.

Wild wolves captured on camera in Oregon

Researchers fit radio collars to wolves to track them in the wild

OR-7'S JOURNEY
NORTHERN CASCADES
PORTLAND
COLUMBIA RIVER
MT. HOOD
OREGON
DESCHUTES RIVER
EUGENE
BEND
Pacific Ocean
CRATER LAKE
ROGUE RIVER
SISKIYOU NATIONAL FOREST
KLAMATH FALLS
MT. SHASTA
CALIFORNIA

WASHINGTON
ZUMWALT
PRAIRIE
N
O
G
WALLOWA
MOUNTAINS
STRAWBERRY
MOUNTAINS
SNAKE RIVER
IDAHO
HIGH
DESERT
MALHEUR NATIONAL
FOREST
0 25 50 75 100
N
W
E
S
GREAT
BASIN
NEVADA

ABOUT WOLVES

SPEED • Although wolves can sprint up to forty miles per hour, their true strength is distance running. They can cover thirty to sixty miles a day. When pressed, a wolf can run a hundred miles in a single day! They are not deterred by rough terrain, fences, steep slopes, bodies of water, injuries, or weather of any kind.

COMMUNICATION • Wolves communicate with each other not just with their voices but also through body language and facial expression. They have a keen sense of hearing, picking up sounds from up to ten miles away.

SIZE • Wolves are four and a half to six and a half feet from nose to tail. Their average weight is 70 to 115 pounds. Males are larger than females, and wolves in the Arctic are the largest of all.

TEETH • Wolves have forty-two teeth—that's ten more than humans! Their bite is stronger than a lion's, a tiger's, or a grizzly bear's. Wolves eat fast—they can gulp down twenty pounds of meat in just a few minutes, equivalent to a hundred hamburgers!

SMELL • Wolves can smell prey more than two miles away. They mark their territory with regular placement of urine, to warn other wolves to keep their distance. Wolves have scent markers in their paws, so that one wolf can follow another.

WOLF TRACKS

• Only a bear's track is larger than a wolf's. Any track that is as large as your outstretched hand belongs to a bear or a wolf. Bear tracks have five toes; wolf tracks have four. The track shown on the right-hand page is life-size.

WOLF PACKS

• Wolves live in packs as small as two wolves and as large as thirty, but most packs have five to eight wolves. A pack is led by an alpha pair that has formed a long-term bond. Some wolves stay in their home pack forever. Others leave and join a neighboring pack. Some, like OR-7, disperse and form a new pack in a new territory.

• Wolf pups are born in the spring. They weigh one pound at birth and have blue eyes that usually turn amber by eight months of age. Members of the pack will drag large pieces of meat back to the den for the alpha female to eat while nursing her pups. Later, adult pack members will carry meat in their throats and bring it to the pups, who lick the adults' mouths to get them to cough up the prechewed meat. Wolf pups reach adult size at one year and they are old enough to disperse from their pack in their second or third year.

WOLF BEHAVIOR

A single wolf pack claims a territory with enough food to feed all its members. A pack will have a regular rendezvous site within its territory where the wolves gather and sleep. The alpha female digs a den for the pups nearby. Territories can be as small as twenty-five square miles. In the Arctic, a pack might keep a five-hundred-square-mile range. Most packs have a territory of about a hundred square miles.

Wolves hunt ungulates, which are animals with hooves, such as deer, elk, moose, and bison. By hunting together, wolves can bring down animals that weigh five to fifteen times more than a single wolf does. To their credit, elk fight back, and many wolves have sustained multiple broken bones from being kicked by their prey. Wolves will take smaller prey when larger game are scarce, and sometimes they eat carrion. They have never hunted humans. Wild wolves have a very strong instinct to hunt what they were taught to hunt by their parents, so most will take livestock only as a last resort.

Working as a pack, wolves hunt prey much larger than themselves

Ravens and wolves are symbiotic; they often work together in the wild to catch prey. Ravens spot prey and lead wolves to it. Wolves open the hides of their prey—something ravens, which lack hooked beaks, cannot do for themselves.

THE HABITATS OF THE PACIFIC NORTHWEST

Journey passed through some of the most spectacular landscapes in the Pacific Northwest, including the Zumwalt Prairie, the wetlands of the Malheur National Wildlife Refuge, and the Rogue River–Siskiyou National Forest.

PRAIRIE

The Zumwalt Prairie is 300,000 acres of the last native bunch grass prairie in North America.

Because it's in a remote area and has an elevation of 3,500 to 5,500 feet, it has never been farmed. In July, it can reach 100 degrees by noon, but fall to 35 degrees overnight. The Zumwalt Prairie is home to many birds, from the smallest song sparrows to the mighty golden eagle. Its grasses and wildflowers support cattle and sheep, mice and voles, deer and elk, coyotes and cougars, and more than a hundred species of bees.

Hells Canyon borders the prairie to the east. At more than 7,900 feet, it's deeper than the Grand Canyon.

Elk are the noisiest of all ungulates: they bark, chirp, squeal, mew, whistle, and bugle. The bulls grow a new set of antlers every spring that can weigh as much as forty pounds, and they shed them every winter. At an inch a day, antlers are the fastest-growing kind of bone.

Coyotes are half the size of wolves, but in many ways they are the more successful predator. They live twice as long, will eat almost anything, and can survive in every climate from the desert to the Arctic, and even the biggest cities.

Hummingbirds are the jeweled acrobats of the bird world. They can hover and fly in any direction, including backward, at speeds up to forty-five miles per hour! They weigh about as much as a penny. They make nests of grass, leaves, and spider silk that are the size of half a walnut shell and hold one to three eggs. Hummingbirds eat twice their weight in nectar, pollen, insects, and tree sap every day.

The mild-mannered, plant-eating **porcupine** is armed with thirty thousand quills. When attacked, porcupines strike with their tails or even charge backward into a predator. The quills embed in the predator's flesh and detach from the porcupine, who escapes. The quills are extremely painful and difficult to remove.

The **Camas plant** has a beautiful purple flower. It's one of the staple foods of the native peoples of the Northwest. When slow roasted, the root becomes a sweet starch that is highly nourishing.

THE GREAT BASIN

In most watersheds, the water runs from the mountains outward to the ocean. In the Great Basin, which encompasses most of Nevada, the western half of Utah, bits of Oregon, Idaho, and California, and a tiny part of Wyoming, the water runs inward and feeds lakes, wet meadows, and seasonally flooded marshes.

The Malheur National Wildlife Refuge is a wetland in the northwestern corner of the Great Basin. It was created in 1908 to protect cranes and egrets from plume hunters, who killed hundreds of birds to collect only a few of the fanciest feathers. At 290 square miles, the Malheur Refuge is one of the largest protected wetlands in North America and is a very important habitat for birds on the Pacific Flyway. Thousands of birds, representing hundreds of different species, visit the refuge. They come from as far north as the Arctic Circle, and as far south as the rain forests of South America. The refuge is also home to deer and pronghorns, coyotes, weasels, mink, porcupines, and badgers.

Wild horses live in two types of herds—a family herd, led by a mare and defended by a stallion, or a bachelor herd, made up of young males turned out of their family herd by the stallion. To rejoin a family herd, a bachelor must defeat the stallion. Female horses form lifelong bonds with the other mares in their herd.

Pronghorns have lived in North America for 20 million years. They are neither antelopes nor deer; their prongs are permanent, like a horn, but they shed the outer covering each year, like an antler. Only the cheetah runs faster than a pronghorn's fifty-five-mile-per-hour sprint. And unlike cheetahs, these herds can run at half their top speed for many miles.

Sandhill cranes are as tall as a seven-year-old and have a wingspan of more than seven feet. They have scarlet caps and traffic-light yellow eyes. They dance, leaping into the air with spread wings, bowing, honking, hissing, and tossing sticks into the air. They dance to defend territory, to threaten a predator, to find a mate, to teach the young, and to strengthen their lifelong pair bond.

FOREST

The Rogue River–Siskiyou National Forest is the most botanically diverse of all America's national forests. Here, the Mediterranean-style climate of California meets the temperate rain forests and deciduous forests to the north. Great Basin plants from the eastern border also flourish in some areas. Weather patterns from the Pacific Ocean bring 80 to 120 inches of rain a year to the western side of the Siskiyous. The rain shadow gives the eastern slopes 70 inches of rain or less each year. The Siskiyou National Forest rises from sea level in the west to nine thousand feet at its highest point. The world's tallest pine, a ponderosa, can be found here: it can grow up to 270 feet!

The Rogue River watershed has more than two hundred square miles of wild and scenic rivers, which are home to salmon, steelhead, and trout.

Cougars, also known as mountain lions, are nothing like African lions. They don't have manes or live in prides, and they can't roar. But they are brilliant stealth hunters, able to jump more than fifteen feet into a tree, bring a deer to the ground in one pounce, and break its neck with one bite.

Chinook salmon are born in freshwater streams. They swim hundreds of miles to the ocean and thousands more to the Gulf of Alaska, where they grow to as much as 120 pounds. They are the largest of all salmon species, and a favorite food of orcas and sea lions. The survivors return to their home streams to spawn.

The **Western red cedar** can grow for thousands of years. Its wood is easily worked, yet extraordinarily durable. It is used to make canoes, totem poles, houses, and tools. The bark can be made into baskets, clothing, and rope. Many parts are used as medicine. It provides food for elk, deer, and rodents, and homes for owls, swifts, and bears. No wonder the tribes of the Northwest call it the Tree of Life.

Author's Note

Migration is the heartbeat of the world. Many creatures move from one place to the other, from the monarch butterfly that weighs less than half a raisin and flies more than three thousand miles, to the gray whale that travels just as far and weighs forty tons. Animals migrate to find food and shelter; they migrate to give birth to their young. They migrate when another animal threatens their home ground and when their home becomes too crowded. They migrate because of climate change, because humans have taken over their territory, and because of natural disasters like floods, storms, earthquakes, and wildfires.

Humans migrate, too, and for many of the same reasons. We migrate to find work, food, and shelter; to escape war and natural disaster; to be closer to the people we love; and to live in safety and freedom. I hope my wolf's story will resonate with readers who have been uprooted from a familiar place and are trying to find their way to a new home. I am grateful to all the people who extended a warm welcome to me when I lived far from home, and I am even more grateful to people from all over the world who have moved to my home state and made it a richer and more interesting place.

Resources for Young Readers

Documentaries:
How Wolves Change Rivers (Sustainable Human; Chris Agnos, editor) 4:17 minutes
https://www.youtube.com/watch?v=oSBL7Gk_9QU

The Rise of Black Wolf (National Geographic Wild)—45 minutes
https://www.nationalgeographic.com.au/tv/the-rise-of-black-wolf

Books:
Gagne, Tammy. *Gray Wolf,* Back from Near Extinction series. (Core Library, Abdo Publishing, 2017).

Patent, Dorothy Hinshaw. *When the Wolves Returned: Restoring Nature's Balance in Yellowstone.* (New York: Bloomsbury USA, 2008).

Smith, Emma Bland and Robin James. *Journey: Based on the True Story of OR7, the Most Famous Wolf in the West.* (Seattle: Little Bigfoot Books, 2016).

Websites:
National Geographic Education. "Wolves: Fact and. Fiction."
https://www.nationalgeographic.org/media/wolves-fact-and-fiction

National Park Service, Yellowstone. "Wolves."
https://www.nps.gov/yell/learn/nature/wolves.htm

Wolf Conservation Center. https://www.nywolf.org

International Wolf Center. https://www.wolf.org

General Resources

Books:
Blakeslee, Nate. *American Wolf: A True Story of Survival and Obsession in the West.* (New York: Broadway Books, 2017).

Websites:
Oregon Department of Fish and Wildlife. Up-to-date information on all the wild wolves in Oregon and a gallery of trail camera pictures in the public domain.
https://www.dfw.state.or.us/Wolves/index.asp

Oregon Wild. Hosts many resources, including teaching guides and a fact sheet in Spanish.
https://oregonwild.org/wildlife/wolves

Acknowledgments

I am grateful to the many people who helped me bring this story to the page. John Stephenson of the U.S. Fish and Wildlife Service, who tracked OR-7 on his remarkable journey, and the writer and wildlife expert Gary Ferguson both helped me understand the intricacies of wolf behavior. The Outpost writers' workshop at Fishtrap gave me the opportunity to camp for a week on the Zumwalt and learn about the area in depth. Many thanks to my talented and tenacious agent, Fiona Kenshole, and to the creative team at Greenwillow—Virginia Duncan, Sylvie Le Floc'h, Tim Smith, Lois Adams, Laaren Brown, Robert Imfeld, and Ann Dye. I am very grateful to Mónica Armiño, whose breathtaking art makes this book so much more beautiful than I could make it on my own. And finally, to my own packmates: Bill, Monica, Brian, Colette, and Madelaine—thank you for coming along on this journey.